KINGFISHER

Rozie Kelly

Saraband

Published by Saraband
3 Clairmont Gardens
Glasgow, G3 7LW

Copyright © Rozie Kelly 2024

All rights reserved. No part of this publication may be reproduced, stored in a retrieval system, or transmitted, in any form or by any means, electronic, mechanical, photocopying, recording, or otherwise, without first obtaining the written permission of the copyright owner.

ISBN: 9781916812352

Printed and bound in Great Britain by Bell & Bain Ltd, Glasgow

10 9 8 7 6 5 4 3 2 1

For Dad. You would've hated this book.

1.

I can pinpoint, almost to the second, when I realised I wanted to fuck her. It wasn't the first time I saw her in the hallways of the university, nor was it when I first saw her read, and watched her face move from awkwardness to elation. It was a more happenstance occasion than that.

We'd tripped over one another while trying to buy coffee, me drifting, as usual, her clearly on the way to somewhere. But she stopped, as I did, awkwardly holding her coat and bag and some food shopping. It seemed rude not to invite her to sit with me, especially with the sun shining, as it was that moment. We perched on a recently vacated bench by the river. The ducks were fighting over crusts thrown by a small child and his mother. It was spring, so they were filled with its verve and aggression, trying to drown one another, mallards chasing females absentmindedly, flapping and splashing. An elderly cocker spaniel waded nearby, paying them no mind.

Ducks are evil, I said, as I rolled a cigarette.

The world must be very black and white, for you, she said.

It struck me as an odd thing to say, especially in England, where everything is grey. But it was then that I realised I wanted to be inside her. To push her down, to render her imperious intelligence stupid with the weight of my body, with my younger, harder form. I could tell, of course, that she wouldn't accept being dominated, but it was a pleasant thought. She smelled like toast and marmalade. Like wet leather. Yes, I wanted to fuck her. And I don't want to fuck women very often.

I was new to the area, then, although I feel old to it now, despite it being not much more than a year ago that this happened. My memory of that day is potent, but it's blurred, like the feeling of emerging into a bright afternoon after unexpectedly quick pints. Vivid, but indistinct.

I can see the path underfoot as I walked away from her, having finished our coffees, with two Lotus biscuits in my pocket. She'd given me hers. I don't like them, but I took it anyway, and allowed them to crumble in my pocket over the coming days as some kind of reminder. There was toadflax growing in the cracks of the walls, which I gazed at more than where I was going, as I am wont to do, when I am distracted.

I went home to Michael, perhaps earlier than he was expecting me. Or rather, not perhaps, but definitely, because as I stepped into the bedroom (the first room off the hallway of our new flat) he slowly and sheepishly moved some lubricant and a box of condoms from the bedside table and into the drawer. So. There was that. He was having his own fun. More classically consummated than my coffee and imaginings, clearly. But that was the arrangement.

Michael is a beautiful man. There is no denying that fact. He has black hair and blue eyes, a combination I'd believed only fictional until we met. But there he was, clear as day. Sat on the bed in his boxers with a thin gleam of sweat on his smooth chest.

I didn't expect you back yet, he said.

Clearly, I said, with more venom than I'd intended.

We did say ——

Ignore me. I have a headache.

You need to drink more water.

I know, don't start with that.

Michael has a very smooth face. He has never been able to grow a full moustache and beard, although he keeps hoping it will arrive. At 36 years old I would imagine he's missed his chance. He has some soft black hairs in the centre of each cheek, islands that the tides just won't cover.

The smell of glue was emanating from the living room. His other passion. Michael builds model aeroplanes. A hobby he is entirely too beautiful for. His father was in the RAF (one thing we had in common) and instead of finding porn, should I ever open his laptop, I am likely to find strange forums from an earlier, more crudely built version of the internet. Elderly men trying to find one another. Has anyone heard from Billy-Bob '56? Jimmy? Fairy Fred? Snowdrop '62? I'm tempted to write about them but it feels too sad.

We'd decided to sleep with other people a few months previously. He seemed to be making the most of this arrangement, which galled me, but the arrangement itself was a mutual one. I wanted Michael to be in my life long-term. I believe he felt the same about me. We both knew we couldn't be everything to each other. So, we'd made the decision. My frustration stemmed from how much the little fucker got laid. Or rather, how much I didn't. And now I was mysteriously interested in a woman seventeen years my senior. A woman! What was the world coming to?

2.

Michael and I have very little in common. So little, in fact, that it has become something of a running joke between us. One of those jokes you get in relationships a couple of years deep, a joke that's had all the hard edges scuffed off it, that you can settle into like an old sofa.

We bond over music. Have bonded, from the beginning. Our first date was a gig, which I was unsure of at first. It seemed to me an unsociable thing to do – it involved looking at something other than each other, experiencing something other than each other. But then I have always demanded a lot of attention. It's likely that I found some masochistic joy in this beautiful man essentially ignoring me and staring at a stage all night, but also, I found a purer joy in watching him. His whole body moved fluidly to the sounds that filled the air. He bought us cheap beers without looking at the bar staff, he danced broadly and unashamedly for the supporting band, despite initially being the first to move into that wide, cavernous space. He is not a wallflower. He is not a flower at all. He is fire, an explosion, a spark hitting a stream of spilt petrol, the fissure in a sheet of ice before it breaks, the creak before an avalanche – a natural force that's impossible to resist. He was the very first person to teach me that I could forget, however temporarily, what others might think of me, and just exist. I think perhaps Michael enjoyed the opportunity to introduce me to another version of myself. With him I became looser, my corners softened and blurred. I could see the joy he took in watching this happen, watching himself dissolve some of the starch ironed into my very core.

The woman I wanted to fuck is a poet. I met her at the university, whilst in my short position as writing fellow for the MA students – just the spring term. I'd been excited by the position, prompted by the publication of my first pamphlet, not because I cared much about the students, but because I wanted to meet the staff. To rub shoulders with some real writers and thinkers in a non-subordinate scenario. Of course, we weren't equal, but I wasn't having to submit my own poems to their sharp eyes, which felt better. A step closer. She was the big-name writer on the course. The one they put in all the brochures. I'd only heard of one of her books, but then, judging by the distinctly female studentship, I probably wasn't her target demographic. She ran a not-for-credit class each week, which she'd allowed me to sit in on, rather ruining the illusion that I wasn't being taught, but there we are.

Most of us are poets, she said. It's just a question of how it comes out.

She has green eyes and a soft Southern-Irish accent. Smile lines crease her cheeks, and her eyebrows are slightly wild. She looked right at me as she said it, and it felt like an accusation. Like I hadn't yet figured out where my poetry came from.

After our meeting by the river, I began to pay more attention to her. I observed her routine. Most of the other academics passed me like ghosts, if I saw them at all. I understood that they spent their lunches, if they took them, tucked away in their tiny offices. But she was different. She took a break at 1pm every day, on the same bench on campus, underneath a large tree and facing the greenest space the university had to offer. I began to copy her. Eventually, I began to join her.

She would always buy grainy salads from Marks and Spencer. Small bottles of mango smoothie or iced coffees. Such a waste of money. I took curries and chicken and rice from home. Heated them in the dirty microwave. Of all the writers at the university, hers is the work I'd been least interested in. She was always writing about nature, making obscure references to long-dead tomes. Always banging on about birds. Having spent some time with her, it became clear that this wasn't an affectation – she stared at the birds wherever she went. She taught me how to tell when a pigeon is happy. Not something I'd ever imagined caring about, but these days I watch for them dipping and swirling, catching currents in the air for short, joyful moments. A modern-day ornithomantist, then. I write about smells and steel and semen. It took me longer than it should have to realise that we write about the same thing.

That night, after our first coffee, after returning home to Michael, I cooked steaks. For once I'd braved the butcher – normally I can't handle the smell. I didn't make a sauce. I wanted to taste blood. Although it's not actually blood, is it? It's myoglobin. The protein that delivers oxygen to the muscles. I think my muscles needed oxygen. A release of some kind. A deep breath out.

You keep fucking everyone else, I said, over dinner with my mouth full.

He smiled wryly but didn't say anything.

When will it be my turn?

Still quiet, he reached over and took my cock in one hand, through the thin fabric of my jogging bottoms.

When you stop wearing these old things, perhaps?

Never, I said.

He blew me later that night. Nobody wants apology fellatio, do they? I mean, it's still better than no blow job at all, but it's hardly exciting. I could see myself in the mirror in the wardrobe door. I looked terribly sad, although I didn't feel it. I wasn't feeling very much of anything. Most of us are poets? What does that say about everyone else?

3.

The following day I was at the university. I'd been given a strange, draughty office in one of the older buildings. The room itself was shaped almost like a corridor, with a desk at either end, one for me, one for the fiction fellow, who never seemed to be there. It was almost impossible to find, as it involved going up and then down some stairs, so I was constantly fielding emails from latecomers, and opening the door to breathless red faces and gasped apologies. Despite my initial reticence, I found I liked most of the students. I wasn't teaching classes, and it was voluntary for them whether they came to see me or not, which meant that the ones I did see were the earnest ones. The ones who put the hours in. This didn't necessarily mean they were talented – although some were – but it did mean they were serious about being there. They sent me their little poems like paper ships onto a rough sea, and I did my best to try and help them dry out.

There was one girl in particular, though, who irritated me beyond belief. Short, bespectacled, loud-voiced, and obstinate. I suppose I shouldn't call her a girl really; she could only be a few years younger than me, but something about how she sat upright in her chair with her arms wrapped around her folder of empty words didn't allow me to ascribe to her the title of woman. Which I'm sure makes me a cunt.

Her work was all sounds, there wasn't a shred of beauty to be found anywhere. As much as she made me itch, sat there all self-important, she did teach me something. Poetry should be beautiful, I decided. What an extraordinarily mundane thing to realise. I think my favourite poems are the ones that force you to see the beauty in something filthy and used up.

After a long and tiring meeting with The Girl, I went outside into the sunshine and sat on the glossy metal bench where the poet liked to eat her lunch. She came and joined me soon enough. She was wearing an ankle-length dress with a silver belt around her tiny waist. She looked like she worked in an expensive boutique. She looked like a hummingbird. Today she was eating something with green beans and goat cheese. It smelled of lemons.

How are you finding it? she asked.

Finding what?

Well, the job of course.

What do you do when you don't like your students?

I teach them anyway.

I was circling her. I don't believe she noticed. She was always so deep in her work; she seemed surprised when I appeared on the bench every day. Perhaps she is not used to the kind of attention I was giving her. Perhaps she has experienced too much of it. She was in high demand. I was a beggar. I knew she had a purse full of gold, if only I could get close enough to cut the strings.

I think Michael noticed the difference. I was lighter, and this made him happier. He wanted me to be happy but he didn't want it to be any work. At the beginning I tried not to be work. In fact, I worked incredibly hard at it. I was so easy going I felt like I might slip through the floorboards at any moment and disappear. He liked me better like that. But time goes on and it gets harder to pretend, doesn't it? Perhaps love is still being willing to try.

You're quite dangerous, really, aren't you, said the poet.

She was eating spaghetti carbonara, and she sucked a piece of pasta up between her lips, fast, how I'd imagine a cat would do it, if a cat were to eat pasta.

What do you mean? I said, picking at my plate. My fingertips smelled of meat.

Charisma is deadly.

It is?

Yes. And you're an expert at making people feel good about themselves.

Why is that a bad thing?

It's not, exactly. But it's potent. If you can make someone feel good about themselves, you can make them do what you want. They say psychopaths are very charismatic.

Who does?

People do.

She took a swig of her Sauvignon. I mulled it over. This was our first meeting past sundown. She'd agreed to meet me to discuss my new (imaginary) collection. I hadn't been able to come up with a better excuse to see her. Now she was here with me she was softening like butter. It was raining outside, and the windows of the small Italian restaurant were steamed up. I felt tightly wound, like there was a coil of metal in my stomach. It felt like being there was a betrayal, although of what I couldn't say. Our plates were cleared, and the poet ordered a tiramisu before the waitress could go back to the kitchen. When they brought it, she gave a little wiggle of delight. I felt myself harden. On a whim I ordered an Irish coffee, and then watched as the manager came down from the office to show the waitress how to make it. It took her two goes and by the time she brought it over, the poet had eaten her dessert. I realised we hadn't spoken that whole time.

Are you married?

No, she said. I was. But he was profoundly disappointing. Are you?

No, I replied, and didn't elaborate.

When we said goodbye, it was so ridiculously cinematic and beautiful that it made me embarrassed. Not the interaction, you understand, but the environment. Stepping from the steamy restaurant and into the rain, sheltering her under my large blue golf umbrella. Her hair curled behind her ears in the damp. She leaned in and gave me a one-armed hug goodbye. At the last second, she turned her head and kissed me on the cheek. I had forgotten what it felt like to kiss someone who was smaller than me. Although I didn't kiss her, I suppose, I was the recipient.

She smelled like jasmine. No, not exactly. She smelled like the earth beneath a jasmine plant on a hot day. We hadn't talked about my poems.

She didn't join me for lunch for the rest of that week. I sat in the sun eating my overcooked curries and trying not to look around me too much. Students gathered on the grass, laughing, performing youth for one another. I smoked more than I usually do, and I'd been doing so well at cutting down. Not seeing her felt like having too much caffeine.

I was short with Michael that week, in the evenings. He was short back, punching me on the arm and asking me what my fucking problem was. I told him I didn't know, and he accepted it. His fist left a small bruise and I rubbed it with my thumb as I thought about her. He made spaghetti carbonara one night, and ate his like a dog, not a cat, which made me very angry, although naturally I couldn't explain why. But he let me fuck him afterwards, for a change. I kept catching sight of myself in the mirror again. At this rate I should just find a pond and drown myself in it.

4.

That weekend we went to see my mother. Even as an adult man being close to my mother sends adrenaline coursing through me. I so quickly become a small boy again it's as if nothing has changed. My knees and palms begin to ache as if the old wounds are trying to open themselves for her.

My mother lives in sheltered accommodation in a converted manor house. The whole building is covered so thickly with ivy that you can only see the windows. She doesn't like me to see her in her room, she says it makes her feel like she's hospitalised, so Michael and I wait in the communal living room. There are two grandfather clocks and a mantle clock, all running at slightly different times. They tick loudly and out of speed, making it feel like we are part of a Lewis Carroll storyline. I keep expecting to see rabbits. Every hour the cacophony of mismatched tolling bells sets off all the resident's hearing aids, screeching into their deadened ears. The living room is so thickly carpeted that the carers strain to push their missives' wheelchairs through the deep pile.

My mother is a homophobe. Despite this, she and Michael get on wonderfully well. She always did relish having someone to criticise me with. I am frightened of my mother. Michael doesn't know this. I'm not sure whether Michael realises anyone is frightened of anything. He is so completely secure. On this visit, she was wearing a lemon-yellow suit, altered so that she could pour her mishappen shape into it. She smelled like TCP and Angostura bitters. She never smells of anything else. The nurse pushed her to us silently through the thick carpet.

I'll take a tea dear, my mother said to the nurse.

That's not my job Hetty, you know that. Your lovely son can get you one.

Yes, a tea dear, and nice and strong this time. I don't know what it is with you lot here and making weak tea. I should complain.

The nurse rolled her eyes at me and abandoned my mother's chair by our table. It made me want to laugh loudly, so instead I stared at my feet like a little boy.

Hello Hetty, said Michael.

Hello, Michael dear. How is the business?

Booming, actually. Most of our January flakers have stayed on this year. Or are paying us still at least. I'm thinking of opening a new location too.

You'll rid us of those nasty fatties, won't you?

I'm trying my best.

Michael owns two gymnasiums. The sort of gyms that have never had someone with more than 2% body fat step through their doors. But he's placating her. I'm not sure when she last looked in a mirror, as her fast-extending waistline is threatening to overflow her wheelchair these days.

Homophobe. Hypocrite.

Hello Mum.

You look sallow, son. Michael, he hasn't been drinking enough water, has he?

He hasn't Hetty. I do try and tell him, but he won't listen to me.

And you're still living in sin, are you?

Yes Mother, I said.

She can hardly even be bothered these days. Not like the leathering she gave me when she found my magazines. Although she wasn't in a wheelchair, then, admittedly.

It was an enormous relief when the poet joined me on the bench the following Monday. I breathed a heavy sigh as she sat down, and she looked askance.

What?

Nothing. I'm working on my breathing.

Of course you are.

I was surprised to see her take out a Tupperware. In it was a jacket potato with tuna, some coleslaw and salad.

No M&S today?

I'm working on being *organised*.

She said it as if it were a made-up word. As if she was trying it out for size.

We still need to talk about your collection, she said.

I'd like that.

You should come for dinner.

She wrote down her address for me on a piece of paper, which was the one time I'd really considered the fact of our age difference as a potential issue.

I have a flat in the city, where I stay when I'm working during the week. I'll cook. Are you free on Friday evening?

I am.

Eight okay?

Absolutely.

Good.

She began to eat her jacket potato. That day she smelled like linen and hope.

On Sundays Michael cooks all our lunches for the week. He makes a huge pot of curry, grills endless chicken breasts, steams brown rice. He lays out all our Tupperware in symmetry on the counter. He weighs everything and tries to tell me about macronutrients or some such nonsense.

When I get back from playing squash, he asks me – have you taken your electrolytes?

Salt, Michael, I say. It's just a fancy word for salt. I'm not a fucking hamster.

You're my hamster, he says, and gives me two tablets.

One day I'm going to crush them up in front of him and sprinkle them on my dinner.

This week he tells me he misses me.

You see me every day, I tell him.

That's not what I mean, he says.

Michael makes me feel peaceful. We have a routine. He's up early to train (he works out at a different gym, rather than his own, which always struck me as odd). He makes the tea and brings me a cup in bed. I often wake to its cold presence on the bedside table, knowing that he left hours ago. After he has been to the gym, he comes home, showers, and sits in his office doing paperwork. By this time I've surfaced, and I make our coffee – freshly ground, a new blend each week, purchased at the farmer's market. He smells of the minty shower gel he uses, and always kisses my hand when I put down his mug. We both drink our coffee black. Another of the few things we have in common. When I try to imagine us growing old together, I cannot picture his face, but I can smell mint and feel him kiss the back of my hand.

After our coffee and my shower (I don't think I've showered once in that flat without the glass being steamed up from Michael), I leave for the university. I am technically not required in the office for more than three days, but I go in for five. The corridor-office isn't used by anyone else, and, although cold, is quiet and conducive for my work. Or so I tell myself, to avoid the fact that really, I want to eat my lunches on that metal bench. I have started buying mango smoothies and iced coffees from M&S. I can see what the fuss is about. I let them rim my mouth with their sweetness.

I am trying to write a poem about birds. I know, I know. Don't. They're not real birds, at least. I want to write about a water fountain in Stratford-upon-Avon, where I grew up. The fountain is shaped like two metal swans, wings open, facing each other. Perhaps in conflict, perhaps edging on a human embrace, who knows. I like how sharp the swans are. They look dangerous. Hetty thought the statue was a monstrosity when it was first put up, which may have contributed to how much I like it. Every line I write feels trite, predictable. Maybe I should write about a hamster instead.

So. Dinner with the poet. You must be wondering. I'd spent my day in that draughty office, writing terrible lines about stiletto blade swans and such. What rubbish. I was angry and horny and most of all I was hungry, although it was the kind of hunger where you don't realise until it makes you feel ill.

The poet's flat was in a suburb of the city and comprised of the basement and ground floor of a pretty (large) Victorian house. It irritated me but I'm not sure why. People with money are irritating but then I'm one of them so who am I to talk? I rang the doorbell and took a few deep breaths. Why was I letting myself get so worked up? To my surprise, when she answered the door, she was wearing black jeans and a cream silk blouse. Jeans? It threw me. She looked wonderful – sparkling clean and fresh. An advert for fabric conditioner.

Wine? she said, before she even said hello.

I laughed like a big gust of wind. Yes, oh yes, I said.

The flat was beautifully decorated. It had retained its original fireplaces, complete with cobalt tiles. The carpets were hessian and they caught on my socks (it was a shoes-off house). Everything was immaculately clean and quite minimal. With her wild hair and eyebrows and obsession with birds, I think I'd imagined some dark and sumptuous space filled with taxidermy. But I was wrong. There was a watercolour of a swallow on one wall. Or was it a martin? I get them confused.

Here, she said, handing me a large glass of red. She hadn't asked what colour I wanted, and I saw she was drinking white. So, she thought she knew me, then. I suppose she was right too. I took a sip, then another. It was good. Something Italian and hearty, my best guess. Montepulciano d'Abruzzo, perhaps. There was a large Le Creuset on the stovetop, the contents bubbling. It smelled like preserved lemon.

Sit down, she said, gesturing to the breakfast bar. It had a white marble top.

I didn't picture you liking white marble, I said.

I didn't decorate. She smiled ruefully. I bought it like this and have made very little imprint at all. Which is the point, I suppose. I brought books, blankets, and birds. Everything I need to write. And to sleep.

I sat down on one of the tall wooden chairs. It squeaked, which embarrassed me. I realised I didn't know how to talk to her now that we were in her space.

How long have you had it? I asked.

As long as I've been at the university, nearly. So, six years perhaps. I like it.

So do I.

There was a selection of birdfeeders hanging outside the kitchen window. A blue tit was swinging gently as it extracted seeds from one of them. The poet was stirring whatever she'd cooked, but I could see that she had one eye on the feeder the entire time.

5.

She fed me at a large, bleached pine table at one end of the huge living room. There were blue linen placemats and the cutlery looked brand new. We ate moussaka, with some kind of spicy bean stew, and couscous.

Why don't you bring food like this to work? I asked.

I don't cook like this normally. If you weren't here, I'd be eating cereal.

Are you trying to impress me?

I think I might be. Is it working?

Yes.

I thought about her motivations. Was she flattered by me, or did she really want to help me with my writing? It couldn't be that, she must be approached for advice relentlessly. When I put my hand on her forearm she didn't move away. Her motivations were simpler, then.

We drank a bottle of wine each. She made espresso after dinner, and I was grateful. We still hadn't looked at my poems. We drank our coffee by the fire, which she lit, despite it being spring. I was grateful for that, too. It was cold in her minimal house.

Tell me about your partner, she said.

How do you know I have one?

Because I'm not stupid, she said.

Michael is strong, confident. He knows who he is and what he wants in a way I've always been envious of. I think it must be simple, to be him.

I can't imagine feeling that way.

Neither can I.

She seemed warmer after I'd spoken about Michael. She curled her legs up underneath her on the sofa. Her toenails were painted bright green. She'd dropped some kind of guard that she'd been holding so well I hadn't even noticed it was there. She had a tattoo on her ankle, tiny, a bird of course.

It's a yellowhammer, she said, when she caught me looking.

When I was about nine years old, my father took me to a falconry event. I remember being vaguely interested in the birds flying around – and my dad's monologue about the hierarchy of the world, the cruelty of nature and of man, etc etc. I remember being able to smell manure and cigarette smoke. I remember the mud squishing beneath my Spiderman wellies. But what I was really captivated by, what I suddenly remembered while sat in the poet's living room, was the bird at rest.

While my father was smoking a cigar and talking with the management, the falconer, a woman, took me in to see her protegee sleeping. It was in a wooden hut, for some reason slightly too small for an adult to enter comfortably, which made me feel like I was meant to be there. Like it was built just for me. The falconer had to bend forward, as if in supplication. The bird was on its perch, its feathers slightly ruffled. It looked cosy, but alert. Its eyes were open, regarding me with a gentle contempt.

It's awake! I exclaimed to the falconer.

He's watching you, she said, in almost a whisper.

My father liked to hold my hand. He didn't care who saw him be gentle with me, despite his reputation. People thought my father could be cruel and my mother could be kind. How different things can look from the outside. I am frightened of her and her cold fingertips and her moods. Her upswing and her downstream. In my mind my father rides horses and smokes his cigars in a leather chair. In my mind I sit with him.

I stared at him, and he stared at me, this red-tailed hawk. He looked friendly, really, the longer I looked at him. He had a cream eyelid encasing the one chocolatey eye that regarded me, patiently, the other eye cast in shadow. I could see scraps of flesh sticking to his talons, and the gentle rise and fall of his chest – faster than you'd expect for a creature so calm, so still. I hadn't thought about that day for years. The poet watched me with her green eyes. Not chocolatey, true enough, but certainly sharp.

Tell me about your poems, she said, placing her warm hand on my thigh.

I will play the swan, and die in music.
Shakespeare

6.

The poet was releasing a new book. It wasn't a book of poetry, this time, but instead a book of essays. The poet was most famous for her essays, despite the fact that I thought of her as the poet. This book was broadly described as nature writing, but truly it was more personal, more revealing.

She'd allowed me to read one of the essays before the release. It told the story of her breast cancer diagnosis, her complex relationship with the oncologist, her visit to the lab to look at her own cancer cells from a biopsy, under a microscope. She mapped the shape of those flailing cells like a landscape, following the undulating hills as a part of her recovery, her long pilgrimage towards acceptance. She wrote of the double mastectomy that followed, the pain, the dullness, the perceived loss of womanhood. Of seatbelt ache and burning bras – really burning them, in her garden, with friends and wine and toasts goodbye to backache and imprinted flesh. And then she wrote of her body afterward, finally free from poisons running through her veins, free from the ills that tried to cure her. She wrote of learning to love her new silhouette, of standing naked in lamplight looking at herself sideways, examining the lack of familiar curves. It was then I realised that she was a genius. There is some kind of stupid, blunt irony, to my wanting to fuck a woman with no breasts. It's unworthy of her.

The launch was held in one of the theatres affiliated with the university. I tried to dress smartly for the occasion but found that none of my clothes would fit me. It seemed like my body had swelled unusually; I couldn't make anything look right. It was as if my form had suddenly taken on the curves she was now lacking, in some kind of sympathy. I was more nervous than she was, I was sure.

She wore a long velvet dress, cut on the bias, black and svelte, like a stallion. She slicked her lips with a stripe of red lipstick like tribal warpaint, but then wore her round glasses like a child. Watching the people in attendance made it suddenly clear to me how celebrated she was, how well respected. People spoke in hushed whispers and grasped copies of the new book on their laps with white knuckles. The book was called Bridges. I felt like I stood in the middle of one as it crumbled beneath me. When I got home that night, with wine-stained lips and a hammering heart, I discovered that Michael had left me.

The clocks went off just as Hetty was wheeled to me. She wore a lavender-blue cardigan. Her face did not betray any discomfort at the noise. Well, no more of a grimace than usually marked her face.

Where is Michael? she said, when the chimes finally stopped. No hello.

Not here, I replied. I felt exhausted already, as if I'd just run a marathon and now had to chair a council meeting.

Well.

I'm fine –

You haven't fetched my tea.

Her hands were flexing in and out, like an old cat. I wished I could just tip her from her chair and onto the floor, to drown slowly in the thick carpet. I got up and went to the small kitchen to make her a cup. I used two teabags. She annoyed me so and yet I made her tea how she liked it. *I am frightened of her upswing and her downstream.*

The flat echoed in my ears. Not sure why, as Michael hadn't actually moved out his stuff. Just a sports bag of clothes, his laptop, his various chargers. He'd left me a note, because apparently we were now inhabiting a bad film. His terrible handwriting (that I'd once found endearing) was now enough to send me into a rage. I could barely read much of it, but I was able to decipher that he'd met someone else. He thought we were too different, now, although once he'd loved that about us. He missed who I'd been when we first met ... He loved me, but not enough to keep living like this. I screwed up the note and threw it in the bin, then took it out again, smoothed it and stuck it on the fridge. How embarrassing.

I think my biggest problem with the whole scenario was how mundane it all was. I'd fooled myself into thinking that Michael and I had transcended the typical relationship paradigm and created something new, something sustainable. Plus, there's always this pressure in the queer community to be better than the heteros. We have our own freedoms, our own rules. Now my boyfriend had fucked off with another man and left me a note. How pedestrian.

One week after the launch, one week after Michael left, I called the poet. She was in the supermarket and seemed distracted.

I think I need to see you, I said. I hated how it sounded as soon as I opened my mouth.

You sound flustered.

Not the word I'd have chosen.

Come to the flat later if you like. But I have work to do, so I can't lose a whole evening to wine again. Promise me that?

I promise.

The poet was sitting in the garden. She led me to a black metal table with a cushion on one of the matching chairs. She sat on the cushion and gestured to the other seat. There were cigarette butts in an ashtray on the table and she smelled as if she was the one smoking them. That was odd. She didn't smoke and complained when I did so close to her.

What's got into you then? she said. Her little round glasses made me want to cry.

Michael has left me.

I see.

I see?

I was incredulous. Why was she so lacking in emotion? Now was the time for emotions, for all the emotions. I wanted her to see that it was her fault, that she was responsible for Michael's departure, with her beautiful words and white apartment. I could smell metal. I didn't say anything, because obviously all my thoughts were completely insane. She thought we were just friends. Thought she was in the company of a gay man. A desexualised man, to her at least. A modern-day eunuch.

You must be devastated, she said. She seemed like she was very far away, as if she was floating in the clouds somewhere and could only just hear what I was saying.

I am, I said. Or at least, I think I am. I'm not entirely sure how I feel.

Would you like a Horlicks? she said suddenly. I've not had one in years, but I'm sure I have some in the cupboard somewhere. My mother used to make me Horlicks when I was sad.

You're not my mother, I said, for some reason.

She looked at me then, sharply. Her eyes were rimmed with red, as if she'd been crying.

Of course I'm fucking not. I'm your friend and I'm trying to make you feel better.

She led me inside and switched on the kitchen radio. Jacques Loussier oozed from the speakers. Bach, Air on the G String. It made me think of familial lines, and how, if one were inclined, one could write the family tree for pieces of music. Was Bach the great-great-great-grandfather of the sounds that poured into my ears, while the poet heated milk in a saucepan? Or was he the original man, and his seed led to the birth of hundreds of musical babies? I suppose he couldn't be the original. Perhaps he was the Genghis Khan of music, then, fucking his way around all the available pianos. I was spiralling, I could tell. The poet scooped a beige powder into the saucepan and stirred some more. The milk began to bubble. She turned down the heat.

I've never had Horlicks before, I told her.

It's very comforting, she replied.

She took two clay mugs from the cupboard, with a cracked blue glaze spread across their surface. She carefully poured us a mug each and put the empty saucepan in the sink. She turned to face me. Without thinking, I leaned down and kissed her. After a moment, she kissed me back.

7.

I realised that morning that I didn't have anything to bring for lunch. That I would never taste one of Michael's overcooked curries again. The fact made me more upset than the fact of him leaving. More than the idea of not smelling mint shower gel in the mornings.

I'd had my first shower in that flat that wasn't steamed up. I didn't know our boiler was capable of making such hot water. I'd made myself a cup of coffee with milk and sugar, in the staff kitchen once I got to work. Perhaps now I was a man who took milk and sugar? It was too sweet for me, really, but I could learn to like it. A man who was attracted to women, or a woman, at least. A man who lived alone and took milk and sugar in his coffee.

I had two appointments with students that day. One of which was The Girl who irritated me so. The other, a young man who showed promise. His work was messy and sprawling and he did not yet seem to understand the concept of redrafting, but there was beauty there. He wrote about being a brown boy in England, about language and misapprehensions and loss and identity. It was clear to me he should perform his work, and I gave him a list of potential nights he could attend to give it a try. Normally, I'm faintly judgemental about that sort of thing, but everything about the boy was musical – his long limbs, his sloping grace, his lilting voice. People should listen to him, not read him. Perhaps one day he would turn his refrains into songs. He left me buoyed by the experience, and I was reminded of why the job was a good fit. My charisma isn't always psychopathic, sometimes it can be a gift. I don't like the thought of being dangerous, I don't think I've ever intentionally harmed anyone. The poet was under my skin like a parasite. Nibbling away at my understanding of myself.

The second appointment, The Girl, did less for my mood. She'd had one of her stupid sound poems published in a journal that had previously rejected my own work. She confided in me that she'd written the poem based on a list of words she's found online. Her stupid sounds weren't even original. While she talked, I thought about what would happen if I punched her, running through the sequence of events in my head. Eventually, she was done, and I hadn't hit her. I congratulated her, sounding convincing even to my own ears, and saw her out of the door. When she was gone, I wedged a chair under the doorhandle and sat on the floor and cried.

Michael was gone for two weeks. When he came home, he had a deep tan. I arrived back from the office to find him sitting at the kitchen table reading the paper.

Where have you been?

Mexico, he said. He turned the page with a rustle.

Mexico? You're behaving as if that was a normal thing to do.

I put my bag down and took off my jacket. I was aware that I should probably be feeling emotional, but I was very calm. Michael was back, equilibrium had returned.

Michael closed his paper. I know. I'm sorry. The note was foolish, leaving was foolish. I missed you. I want to come home.

But you've met someone else?

Well. It turns out he's pretty foolish too. I realised I can't be with someone more stupid than me. And you are the most intelligent man I know.

Well, I certainly feel wanted.

You are wanted. I want our life. I want to cook for you, I want to sleep next to you.

I should make more of a fuss.

Michael stood up and came over to me. He took my hands and looked at me with those eyes, those remarkable, terrible eyes. He is the human incarnation of a husky.

Can I stay? he said.

Of course you can.

Sometimes it's that simple. Of course it's not really, but I so wanted it to be in that moment that I quieted the noise in my chest. Michael was a beautiful thing in my life, even I could see that.

The following morning Michael poached eggs. The Strokes were playing from the small speaker in the corner of the kitchen. When I went into the bathroom the glass was all steamed up and it smelled of mint. I cleaned my teeth. I was overcome with all the emotion that had been absent the night before. I went into the kitchen and sat down, Michael turned and passed me a cup of coffee. Black.

I take milk and sugar now, I said, petulantly.

I've only been gone two weeks.

I pushed the cup towards him. He took the milk from the fridge and poured me some.

You don't need sugar, he said.

I know. I want it.

Fine. He got it out of the cupboard and put it on the table.

Why Mexico? I asked.

Nicolás is from Mexico.

I think I need you to stop fucking him.

I will.

You will?

I have.

Once Michael returned, I didn't see much of the poet. She did not call me, and I did not call her, and the spring term drew to a close, so there were no more lunchbreaks on the metal bench. I was no longer required in that little office, but I still went in. I needed somewhere that felt like it was just mine. My post had essentially ended, but I was permitted to make myself available until the student's deadlines were up. And the room was not being used. It was quite clear to me from his behaviour that Michael was still seeing Nicolás. He was the big gay elephant in the room. I studiously ignored it. I am not good at confrontation. At lunchtimes I sat hopefully on the bench, just in case.

Finally, in desperation one afternoon (but not desperate enough to call her and ask why I'd heard nothing since the Horlicks incident), I went and sat by the river. I'd bought myself a latte, of all things, and took a seat on the wooden bench, where we'd sat just a few weeks before, and watched the ducks. They were now playing innocent, with strings of ducklings following their mothers merrily. No hint of what they would turn into, or of what had spawned them.

My coffee was hot and sweet. The air smelled of buddleia, of freshly poured tarmac, of the dust on a butterfly's wing. It smelled of damp leaves. Perhaps she would find me here, and we would begin a new routine on a new bench. Perhaps our whole relationship would consist of benches and coffees and sandwiches wrapped in plastic. I wished for her to appear, but she did not. Perhaps I had frightened her, by kissing her? She had considered herself in safe company, and I had proved myself a danger by cupping her chin in my hand and tasting the malt on her lips. She herself had told me that I was dangerous. That I could make people do what I wanted them to. If that were true then she would appear now, but she did not.

Michael wanted to go and see Hetty with me that weekend. To reassure her that he was still around. There was a slight panic in his eyes when I resisted. Michael can be surprisingly conventional at times. Or rather, he has a commitment to appearing conventional to others. The idea of wilfully reassuring my mother of anything seemed foreign and frankly insane to me. But he took his obligation to her very seriously. His mother is such a saint, he thinks I'm being dramatic. *How could anyone be that bad/she's just a product of her time/she doesn't mean it.* That sort of thing. But as I say, I've not told him what she's done. Not really. No use dredging all that up again.

When I told Hetty, as a child of about six, that there were monsters under my bed, she told me I'd better run and jump at bedtime, because they liked the taste of skinny-boy-ankles. She put me to bed earlier, at 5pm, after that, so that she could drink vodka and listen to Wagner. If she thought Michael was gone then all to the good. Perhaps I could justify fewer visits, then. The sun was warm on my back, and I took off my jacket. I closed my eyes and listened to the water. It was peaceful, here, alone. I hadn't felt peaceful for a while. I didn't want to go home.

The poet invited me to an art exhibition with her the following week. She invited me by email, so it was hard to read the exact tone, but she seemed breezy and friendly. Perhaps she was trying to re-establish us as friends, rather than anything more. I imagined her drawing a literal line between us with permanent marker. You stay there, she said in my head, and I'll stay here on my side. *Friends*.

I was delighted to discover that the exhibition was of landscapes in oil and watercolour, from a collective of artists that had settled in a commune in Cornwall in the '60s. I had been concerned that there would be modern art involved, and that my brain would flatline. I just could not make myself care about abstract shapes. The sound-poems of the canvas.

The gallery was small but brightly lit and it echoed in a pleasing way. It smelled of wood varnish and cheap wine, of which the poet had grabbed us each a glass before I arrived. It was busy enough for a buzz, without it being too awkward to move around without bashing into people. Overall, it was what I would consider a perfect date. Except that it wasn't a date, was it? The silence since I had last seen her made that clear to me. That didn't matter, though, as seeing her was as much of a balm as ever. She wore a fitted red jumper, and smart black slacks. Patent leather shoes that I could almost see my face in.

You look good, she said to me. No hello, as usual. She'd stolen my line.

So do you, I replied weakly.

She handed me the wine and I took it, relieved to have something to do with my hands. I clasped it with both of them like a lifeline.

We moved as one from painting to painting. They were all of the same small cove, which one might think would be boring, but it was glorious. Not only were the artists all different in their approach, but the difference in the light, in the tides, in the weather in each of the paintings made me feel as though I was travelling through time. It gave me vertigo and made my hands sweat.

At the back of the gallery was a separate room. It turned out that one of the artists specialised in extremely accurate and detailed images of birds. In particular, the sea birds that are native to that part of the coastline. So that was why we were here. I was overcome with an almost uncontrollable lust as I watched her walk towards the small room with her mouth slightly open. She stood at the doorway for a moment, without going in. A couple were trying to get past us, and she hadn't noticed, she was so transfixed by the birds. I placed my hand on the small of her back to try and steer her out of their way.

She looked at me sharply. There were spots of red high on her cheeks and her lips were stained from the wine in her hand. For once she was drinking red, to match her jumper.

When a man puts his hand on a woman's lower back, it can only mean one of two things, she said, in a low voice, so the couple couldn't hear us.

And what are they? I asked. I left my hand where it was.

He either wants to sleep with her, or to control her. Which is it?

Perhaps it's both, I replied.

She said nothing, returning to look at the birds. But she looked pleased, I thought. My heart was going absolutely berserk the whole time. We didn't say anything else for a long while, and when we did speak again it was to discuss the paintings. She stood for ages in front of one of the painted birds, with her mouth slightly open again. When she went to get us another glass of wine, I purchased it for her. The painting was of a Sterna Paradisaea, an Arctic Tern. A 'Sea Swallow'.

8.

Sometime around then, I can't be sure exactly when, except that it was when I was in the midst of my confusion, of my infatuation, I met my friend Jessica for dinner. I needed to talk to someone I wasn't either sleeping with or trying to sleep with.

Jessica is Scottish, from a wealthy family, so she has one of those delicious accents. BBC Scotland, Scottish RP. Very Kirsty Young. She works in advertising and is so far removed from the world of academia that she's an absolute tonic. I met her when we shared a house in our second year of uni. I did fuck her a few times back then, but then we fell into friendship. She looked after me. Still does, in many ways. I filled her in, for the most part anyway, over tapas.

Polyamory, she said.

What?

That's what it's called now. She took a swig of her drink and elaborately waved at the waiter – a twirl of her fingers – to signal that she wanted another round of the same. Jessica is very good at restaurants.

Poly – many. Amory/amor – love. Many loves. That's what you're doing.

I know what the words mean, Jess, don't patronise me. What happened to a good old-fashioned open relationship, anyway? I can't keep up.

Stop being silly. You're only thirty-five. You say Michael is still seeing Nicolás. You're interested in this poet woman. Polyamory. We'll get onto your mummy issues when more drinks arrive.

Jessica looked very pleased with herself. She leant back in her chair and ate a piece of balsamic-glazed chorizo off a cocktail stick.

Wasn't I supposed to have some kind of say in it, though? I thought the whole point of these new relationship structures is that they are mutually agreed. Michael just fucked off to Mexico and now I have to pretend I'm fine with his new boyfriend. I'm not fine, Jessica.

Yes, I can see that, you're giving yourself new wrinkles. Stop frowning and eat your prawns. And explain to me how it's different – you didn't mind him fucking Nicolás until you realised that they also sometimes go to the cinema together. What's changed, really?

Well. Trust. The trust is gone because he dumped me, didn't he? Then, I assume, decided that finding a new place to live was too much fuss so he came home.

But you love him?

I do.

Then it's the trust that needs to heal. Michael loves you; he does. You two make a lot of sense. Your life together is still a good one.

I suppose.

Now, tell me more about this poet. Let me into your filthy little mind.

I will if you're paying for dinner.

Fair enough.

When she hugged me goodbye, Jessica pressed my face into her big, pillowy tits, as she always did. She liked that it made me squirm. She thought it was funny. This time, I didn't wriggle and pull away dramatically. Instead, I stayed there until all my oxygen had run out.

After a moment, she cradled me more gently. I think she could tell that I needed it. I definitely don't want to fuck Jessica anymore, as brilliant as she is. There is something about the poet in particular, then. Although, as we know, the poet doesn't have any tits. I knew I had it bad, because at that moment I couldn't picture her face at all.

You've changed, Jess said, as she climbed into her taxi.

Oh yeah?

Yeah. You're not such a bitch anymore.

9.

The sun was shining gloriously on my official last-last day in the office. I'd sent the poet a text that morning, on my way in, to say that I'd be on the metal bench, and that this was her last chance to see me there. I hadn't expected anything back, but she responded to say that she'd bring Prosecco and sausage rolls. She could be so unbelievably literal, when all I wanted to do was use code and innuendo. If I wasn't careful, she'd have me communicating properly.

When she arrived, not only had she brought sausage rolls, but she'd clearly raided the closest M&S for a full picnic. She was wearing jeans again, which felt impossible for me to deal with, and her crepe blouse showed glimpses of her freckled shoulders. She seemed happy, stupidly so, but she smelled of copper and bleach, so I was immediately suspicious. More so when she asked me for a cigarette.

I thought you hated them.

I do. But obviously I want to smoke them too.

What changed?

Let's not talk about that. I want today to be a happy day. I don't want to cloud things over with my rubbish.

Nothing you have to say to me could be rubbish.

There you go again.

There I go again what?

I can't figure you out. You're behaving like you want to be with me. You say all sorts of vague things that sound meaningful but aren't. You kissed me when I'd obviously been crying.

I didn't know you'd been crying.

Liar.

I'm not lying. (I was).

I don't know where I am with you and it's exhausting. By my age this confusion is supposed to be over. Now give me that lighter, would you.

That day was the second time I kissed her. I think she was right that I only tried when she was vulnerable. I was frightened of rejection, yes, but also, if I'm honest, I hadn't lied when I'd said I wanted to control her. I wanted to compress this feeling I had when she was around, crush it down into something manageable, something I could carry. Thinking that to myself felt like the most honest I'd ever been. I didn't push her to tell me what was wrong, which I now know I should have. I kissed her on the bench where our colleagues could see us, should they happen to be looking. I didn't know then; how close I was to getting everything I wanted from her.

The train was packed out. Two small children petted a little dog, who got so excited that he weed up their legs. Apologies were exchanged. Baby wipes were handed around. My phone felt slick against my ear.

She knows, Jess. She told me as much.

Well of course she knows.

What do you mean 'of course'? I thought she'd just chalk it up to some stupid joke. I thought she thought I was gay. I thought *I thought* I was gay.

Too much thinking all round, said Jess.

I could hear her pull on a cigarette and exhale heavily through the phone.

You men, you think it's hidden. But you wear it like a colour. When you want to fuck someone it's like you've put on an a-board and you're ringing a bell. We all know.

But howwwwwwww? I wailed.

An old woman sitting across from me shot me a look. Fuck her.

I hadn't had a crisis like this since I was a teenager.

It comes out of your pores. We can smell it.

Having officially left the university now, no matter how much I didn't want to think about it, I needed work. I was lucky, really, that Michael had come back – he was someone who attracted money to his person as if he'd rolled in honey. I am not one of those people. I am one of the sorts of people that racks up lots of credit card debt because they cannot imagine wearing cheap clothes, but also categorically cannot afford expensive ones. I hadn't done that specifically for a while, but I had been letting Michael absorb the brunt of the bills so that I could avoid taking on too much proofing work. He earned enough. And he owed me that much.

I sat at our kitchen table with the wanted ads and a biro. I'm not exactly sure why, except that it made me feel like I was in a '90s sitcom while I drank my coffee (I'd kept the milk but ditched the sugar). I circled a few things for fun and scribbled some notes in the margins. I hadn't written anything at all, not since the farce that was the swan poem. Michael came in and looked over my shoulder.

Going to dance for your dinner?

Maybe, would you like to watch?

I would pay to see that.

I think that's the point.

I got up and shimmied towards him. He took my hand and spun me around. Then he hugged me. I breathed in all his smells, feeling weak. I didn't want him to have another boyfriend. I didn't want to have a girlfriend (not that I did). I wanted him to love me like he had before, and for everything to be different and the same. I mumbled as much into his shoulder. I'm not sure he heard everything I said, but he squeezed me tighter. When I eventually pulled away, he drew me closer for a kiss. That was how it was supposed to be – two faces aligned, like his was with mine. I needed to find a way to focus on Michael. Perhaps if I did that, if I became more present, he wouldn't look elsewhere for connection.

Perhaps if I worked harder at being with him, he wouldn't need to go looking for Nicolás. I needed to cleanse the poet from my mind.

I went for a swim to clear my head. I had all these days stretched out in front of me now, with nothing to fill them with. I should be writing. I should be writing. I should always be writing, and yet, I am not writing. And yet, as all writers know, even the serious ones, we are not actually writing very much at all. Writing is like doing an ultramarathon in the desert, but only for an hour or two a day. We get up, we do whatever inane tasks are required of us that day, before or after we begin to run (write) but ultimately, at some point, we step through a door in our minds and run beneath the burning sun and we sweat and need water and think that we can't do it, that we won't make it. Then we stop, step back into our offices or wherever, go and put the kettle on. We do that most days, willingly, and eventually books and essays and poems and theory exist. For some people I imagine they run in ice and snow. For me it's always hot and arid. Writing makes me feel thirsty. Like a thirsty failure.

I went for a swim to cool myself down after feeling like a thirsty failure staring at a blank page, or worse, trying to redraft the swan poem. I am a member at one of Michael's gyms, because I, unlike him, cannot afford to turn down a free membership. His gyms are immaculately clean and play lo-fi hip-hop that is somehow simultaneously too loud and too quiet. The changing rooms smell like almond-scented cleaning fluid that reminds me exactly of the marble stairs to the apartment we used to stay in when we holidayed in Spain, when I was a child. Marble stairs that were mopped daily by an elderly Spanish woman who would occasionally feed me Tarta de Santiago. Almonds on almonds. I changed into my trunks without looking at my reflection or at anyone else, and almost ran out to the pool and plunged under the surface.

I swam as many lengths as I could manage, fewer than I'd have liked, but I was pleasantly tired. I spent a while alternating between the steam room and a cold jet of water down my back. I wanted to regain control of my body through the switch in temperatures. It didn't work, in that sense. But it did make me feel good. And I hadn't thought about the poet the entire time.

In the changing room, as I opened my locker to get my shower gel, I could feel eyes on me. When I turned around, I vaguely recognised the face in front of me. A young man with curly hair that fought against the water pulling it down. Probably in his late twenties. I had a feeling I'd seen him on one of the apps. Or maybe he just had one of those faces. He had green eyes and a look in them that I hadn't seen for a long while. He didn't say anything, and neither did I, but when he turned and headed for the showers, I felt an excitement in my belly that I'd sorely missed. I felt thirsty.

He pulled me into a cubicle and closed the curtain behind us, turning on the shower. The water was cold, but not cold enough to help control my body. He didn't try to kiss me, which I was glad of, as my recent experiences seemed to have taught me that kissing is where the problems start.

I got onto my knees. I savoured the feeling of the sharp edges of the tiles against my skin. Repentance. That was what I needed. I took him in my mouth and the shower water running over me made me feel as if I were drowning and I thought to myself – wouldn't this be the best way to go?

10.

Perhaps surprisingly, the boy in the shower made me feel much closer to Michael. Less questioning. The simplicity of the exchange, the supplication and reward, the lack of a need to communicate beyond the physical. It made me feel more tranquil and stopped me from worrying about the poet. For a while anyway. I decided to make salmon en croûte for dinner. I knew Michael would have something to say about the calorie content, but I planned on making him work it off later.

When I arrived back with the shopping he wasn't at home. I put the radio on and switched on the oven. I'd bought pastry sheets, so it wasn't much work, but I needed to make the sauce.

Salmon always feels like a treat to me. I have an ex who hated it passionately, and so I lived a salmon-free existence for three years until that particular mistake blew up in my face. I made a resolution to never go without something I enjoyed on behalf of a partner again. It was about time I began to think that way, as Michael certainly had no problem doing so. I kept coming back to what Jess had said – why was it different, now they were dating and not just fucking? I'd put it down to trust, before, but I was no longer so certain that was right. It was more like simple jealousy; that he wanted more than just the body of someone else. But Jess was right. So did I.

When Michael came home, I hadn't finished cooking. I pushed him up against the kitchen counter and kissed him roughly. I felt painfully aroused, unsatiated by the encounter with the boy. Michael kissed me back and pulled my head back by my hair. When he turned me around and dragged my clothes from me, I stared at the pastry sheets on the side, the salmon fillets glistening in their wrapper, the cream sauce bubbling gently on the hob. Michael entwined his arms in mine from behind, so that I couldn't move, even if I'd wanted to. He is so strong. He fucked me slowly while I stared at the ingredients to our dinner.

Afterwards we ate in our underwear, not bothering to tidy the pile of jeans and shirts on the floor. Michael licked cream sauce from my fingers and didn't mention the calories once. I decided I was happy for him to have Nicolás. I watched him humming under his breath as he cleared the table. He seemed so gentle and childlike. I wanted him like this. What was the point if we were not both happy? As we loaded the dishwasher, I could hear the poet's voice. At first, I thought I was imagining it, but then I realised she was being interviewed on the radio about her new book.

I decided it was time to take matters into my own hands. I emailed the poet and asked her out for dinner. I received a strangely formal response. It didn't quite sound like her. She replied saying that she was feeling rather tired, but that she'd love to see me. Would I like to come to her house, her proper house not the flat? She wasn't up for cooking, but we could order from an excellent Thai restaurant in the nearest town. She signed off with her full name, which she'd never done before.

We arranged to meet in a few days, and she sent me her address. I looked it up online, for directions of course, but also a sneak-peek. It was a large, detached property with a huge garden. I couldn't see much more than that, as street-view only allowed me up to the gates. The house was basically in the middle of nowhere. Perhaps this was the taxidermy-filled haven I had expected. By the looks of it I would need to borrow Michael's car, as the journey involved a bumpy road into the woods that I didn't fancy forcing a taxi down. I was perturbed by her email's tone, but I was excited too. I wanted to see her, to smell her. I wanted more than sex from her. I could admit that now.

That week I was in good spirits. I'd picked up some work, proofing funding proposals for a small company in the city. Hardly mentally stimulating, but the day rate was good, and I needed the money. I was hot-desking at a big building in town – free coffee and air con and velvet sofas, all provided by the firm. An old mill building with huge wooden beams. It felt good to have a workspace again, albeit a shared one. I spent a cheerful few days reading boring copy and changing all the flat and confused sentences. I drank lots of free coffee and ate salads, went to the gym daily. I didn't see the boy again, but I was glad of that.

Michael came and met me for dinner after work. We went to a steakhouse and ordered huge dinners. He ate more when he was happy, and became less concerned with reducing food to numbers and fuel. I was buoyed by his mood; he held my hand across the table and made jokes. I was reminded of how Michael could be when he wasn't trying so hard to be someone else. I laced my fingers into his and traced the edges of his palms. I felt peace.

When we first met, Michael only had the one gym. We had an encounter in the changing rooms there, not dissimilar to my recent encounter with the boy, except that I'd misread the situation. He didn't want to lead me to the showers, he'd wanted to ask for my number. He couldn't fuck me in his own gym, he'd laughed, it wouldn't set a good example. I'd been embarrassed, of course, but Michael had been gentle. He was tactile from the off – touching my arms and hands, taking my shirt sleeve between his fingertips as he spoke to me. I gave him my number. Of course I did. Who wouldn't?

At first I'd been unsure what it was he saw in me in return, beyond the physical. But gradually I began to understand how much Michael valued routine, the serenity of routine, and then I realised what I could offer him. Despite my gender I could give him something that appeared like conventionality. I am not conventional myself, I don't think, but I could keep a clean house and fix him a drink and be suitably impressed by his career (which wasn't artificial). I could ensure that the right music was playing when he arrived home, that we had the good coffee well stocked in the cupboard, that the towels were thick and warm and expensive. I offered him the space to relax. I don't think he'd had much of that growing up, particularly in a military family. Once I'd taken this role upon myself I used it to excuse a multitude of behaviours, mine and his.

Our dinner was long and relaxed, and we both drank a couple of whiskey sours. We stumbled home drunk and watched The Florida Project. Sat on the sofa, legs intertwined, the open window letting in the sounds of the street. We didn't have sex that night, instead Michael played me the songs he'd have chosen for the movie's score. I tried to tell him the lack of music was an aesthetic choice, but he wouldn't have it.

Who would choose to be without music? he said, incredulous.

That was the point, I thought to myself. They didn't choose. They didn't get to choose anything about themselves. But I had to admit he was right. And that evening made me think that perhaps Jess was right too. I walked my two fingers over the moles on Michael's shoulder, and he leaned back so that his hair brushed my arm. He smelled like cloves and whiskey. I loved Michael, and tomorrow I would go and see the poet and remember that I loved her too. Or whatever it was that I felt for her.

On the day I was due to have dinner with the poet, I was informed that Hetty had been taken ill. Nothing too serious, we were assured by the care home receptionist who phoned, but she had asked to see us, and she would be bedbound when we came. I was certain she had some ridiculous and unreasonable request for me, but Michael thought she was scared, that she needed our support. Hetty has never been scared of anything in her entire life. Part of me couldn't be bothered to see her, to listen to her rubbish, but another part of me rather relished the prosect of seeing her weakened.

When we arrived at the home, the receptionist phoned upstairs and informed us that Hetty's main carer would be down to see us and would then take us up. I took a mint humbug from a crystal bowl on the counter and sucked on it while we waited. It was cool in the entranceway, and the sofa was comfortable. I wondered briefly whether I could get away with sleeping there while Michael went to see Hetty. She'd be happier to see just him anyway.

The carer was a woman in her forties with tightly braided hair. She was smiling and gentle and I felt an immediate sympathy with her, for having to deal with my mother and her casual intolerance. She didn't introduce herself, but it was the action of a busy woman rather than a rude one.

As you know, Hetty has had an ulcer on her right foot for some time now, she said.

I didn't know this, but I didn't disabuse her, and Michael didn't react at all. It wouldn't surprise me if he did know. I sat quietly waiting for more.

We have been monitoring it and treating it for some time, but it only seems to be getting worse, she said. It's been, ah, complex, getting Hetty to agree to some of the behaviours that would allow her to be more mobile and in less pain. One of the side effects of this is that, aside from allowing us to dress it and keep it clean, Hetty hasn't collaborated with us on her treatment.

The carer pulled her braids together over one shoulder and fell silent, looking at me expectantly.

Yes, I said. The toffee from the humbug glued my teeth together. The carer was trying so hard to be diplomatic about my mother's insistence on dying messily in their hands, and I owed her a response. But I could not muster one.

Well, this has resulted in the ulcer getting worse. Now some of the flesh has begun to die.

I could feel the corners of my mouth trying to twist up. I'm not sure how funny I found it, really, but in the moment, the idea of Hetty literally rotting in this place seemed funny. I'm not an idiot,

I know it's horrible to think something like that. But I couldn't ignore such a perfect metaphor.

What's the prognosis? asked Michael.

I'm afraid Hetty is going to need to have the foot amputated. Understandably she is very upset and frightened. I believe she has asked you to visit to encourage you to stop this from happening. I wanted to see you first to press home how crucial the surgery is. Your mother is not old, she's younger than most of our residents. I would like to see her live a full life, currently she is choosing not to.

Cutting off her foot to spite her face, I said, not quietly enough.

The carer raised an eyebrow but said nothing.

Of course, Michael said, we will explain it to her. She'll have the best care. I have private healthcare, let me know what you require for the referral.

I see, said the carer. She kept looking at me like she expected me to say something, but I just couldn't get any words out. I was trying to imagine what Hetty would look like scared. I couldn't do it. I stood up and brushed my trousers off with unnecessary enthusiasm.

Shall we go up? I said.

I had spent very little time in Hetty's private room. Or rooms, as she had a separate living room and kitchenette. The place cost a fortune and Hetty had been very happy to pick the most expensive options for everything. She was resolute in her opinion that all the money left from Dad's estate belonged to her, and planned on spending every penny before she died, ensuring I would see none of it. Dad would be fucking rolling, except for the fact that he was cremated and sat on her mantlepiece – prime position, I am sure, to watch her disrespect his memory. I hadn't been up there since we had settled her in. At the time she hadn't been assigned a proper wheelchair and spent the first week in her rooms with a walker. She now pretended to be unable to stand, a prophecy that, it appeared, was about to come true.

Although the receptionist had described Hetty's condition as 'bedbound', when we arrived in her rooms she was dressed and seated on the sofa. Her chair was on the other side of the room, and I wondered to myself whether she had been put there or moved herself when she heard we'd arrived.

Hello Dad, I mouthed in the direction of the mantlepiece.

Shall we take a seat? asked the carer.

Michael sat down next to Hetty and took her hand. Her knuckles were swollen like bread in the oven. She cringed when he touched her, but she didn't pull away. Appearances are everything. They had that in common.

This woman is trying to tell me that I need my foot cut off, said Hetty, with no preamble.

She gestured to her right foot, which was tightly bandaged with white gauze. So white it felt blinding, as I stared at it, which I did instead of responding.

My name is Ishia, said the carer. I've seen you almost every day for two years now, Hetty.

I warmed to the carer even more. *Don't take her shit*, I thought. I still didn't say anything. I seemed to have become almost completely mute.

Michael turned so that he was facing my mother and looking right into her eyes. Something I couldn't bring myself to do.

Your diabetes is bad, Hetty. Stuff like this can happen sometimes when we don't take care of ourselves. You must be very frightened.

He squeezed her hand; she yanked it away from him.

Don't patronise me, you little fag. This has nothing to do with diabetes. And I have never been frightened of anything in my life.

I looked over at the bathroom door. Perhaps I could say I needed to use the facilities and go and hide in there until this was all over. As a kid, I used to hide in the bottom of the wardrobe when Hetty was angry. I'd won some glow-in-the-dark stars at the school raffle (a teacher had entered on my behalf, believing, correctly, that I didn't get any pocket money). I'd snuck the stars home and stuck them inside my wardrobe. I liked how they glowed, liked to press my fingertips to them while I waited for the storm to blow over. Michael's shoulders were stiff and pained. I wanted to hug him. I knew so acutely how he felt. I took his other hand in both of mine. I imagined clothes brushing against my face. Quiet, the smell of wood, a hard surface against my back. Still, I said nothing.

Hetty, we don't use language like that here, Ishia said, gamely.

I pay your wages. I'll say what I like.

Regardless of how you may feel about it, Hetty, if you don't have this surgery, you will get very sick and die. Your foot has begun to rot away. It's very important that you understand this and treat it with the seriousness it requires.

The carer looked at me encouragingly, willing me to join in.

I looked down at my shoes.

After driving home from seeing Hetty, Michael headed out to the gym, and I took a shower. I think we both felt the need to wash away the grime of that morning. I'd told him I would be needing the car, and he'd smiled in a gentle but knowing way when he handed me the keys. A certain amount of balance seemed to be returning to us. But, as you might imagine, the encounter at the care home had left me rather rattled and unprepared for my dinner with the poet. For some reason I used Michael's shower gel, and when I got in the car to drive to her house, I realised I smelled like him.

11.

My hands were shaking on the steering wheel. The drive was beautiful, all dappled light from the trees bridging the road, but I found it hard to concentrate on my surroundings. I didn't want to go, really. I wanted to stay at home with Michael and listen to him talk about music. I didn't want to eat Thai food with this woman that I didn't really know, who I definitely didn't know how to relate to.

When she answered the door I could tell, for sure this time, that she'd been crying. She probably wanted me to mention it, but I didn't. I said hello quickly, to get the first word in. It was clear that she'd been drinking – her returning hello was a little slurred and I could smell wine. Good wine. She didn't say much when I entered, just turned, and gestured for me to follow her, muttering something under her breath. The house was cool and quiet. Again, painted in light colours, quite empty and minimal. The artwork from her most famous essay collection, the one that I'd heard of before I started at the university, was framed in her hallway. The sharpness of the orange and yellow looked brighter against the pale walls. I wondered whether she'd decorated the flat that way after all, and had lied to me about it, but dismissed the thought. The hallway opened all the way up to the roof. There was glass everywhere, it was filled with natural light. I couldn't believe that this tiny bird woman lived in such an enormous house, alone. But then, maybe it made sense. It was like an aviary. A façade of openness. A pretence at the sky.

The glass continued, through a long kitchen and out into a conservatory filled with tropical plants. There was a photo of her with Salman Rushdie, somewhere hot. She wore a pale blue silk sari in the photo and her normally freckled skin was lightly tanned. I could see other, important-looking people in the background, and I wanted to stare at it but couldn't do so without her noticing. The poet flopped down onto the wide, cream sofa, and took a swig from an already full wine glass. The condensation from the bottle had made a pool on the table. It was nearly empty.

There are glasses hanging in the kitchen, she said. Or there's some red on the side if you prefer.

It appeared she wasn't trying to impress me anymore. She was clearly drunk.

In the kitchen, I poured us a glass each of iced water from her double-fronted white Smeg fridge. As if she owned such an ostentatious piece of machinery. It was disconcerting. I wanted to know where she was from and what her family were like and where all her money came from. She was successful, yes, but we don't become writers for the cash. I wanted to know who her husband had been and what her parents were like. Did she speak to them? Did they have red hair like hers or were they dark like me? Did she grow up in a house like this, was she raised in an aviary and was that why her feet barely touched the ground as she walked? I didn't know how to ask her any of this, especially now, as she crumbled inexplicably before me.

I took myself an empty wine glass. I decided to drink white too – if nothing else then it would stop her from drinking any more. When I sat next to her on the sofa, I held out the water in front of her face.

Drink, I said.

Whatever, she said, like a teenager. But she took it from me and drank anyway. I waited until she'd glugged the whole thing down before I took it from her.

Do you smoke marijuana? she asked.

Sometimes.

Would you like to now?

If I say yes, do you promise you'll explain to me why you're acting like this?

Oh. That. That'll all come out soon enough. Her face crumpled and she waved a hand around. I can't stop it. I can't stop any of it.

She got up and wobbled out to the kitchen. When she came back, she held a small wooden box, carved, the sort of thing you might buy as a present for a teenage girl. It seemed quite the regression was going on. From it she pulled a thin and immaculately rolled joint and lit it.

Let's order some food. Then I'll stop being so pathetic.

I looked at her green eyes, at the tiny red capillaries, irritated and sore.

You're not pathetic, I said.

What else could I say?

The Thai place is called The Green Elephant. Order us a mix of stuff, and me some hot-and-sour soup?

She curled her feet up on the sofa and handed me her bank card. She seemed better already. She stopped sniffing and took a few deep drags on the joint before handing it to me. It was the first time I'd seen a woman in her fifties smoke weed. It was the first time I'd seen a woman in her fifties cry. I went back to the kitchen to make the call, for some reason not wanting her eyes on me as I did so. When I came back in, she'd somehow composed herself entirely. Her eyes were still red, but her back was straight and she'd smoothed her hair behind her ears. I realised she'd cut it – instead of brushing her shoulders it curled at her jawline. It suited her, and I told her as much.

Don't get used to it, she said. It'll be gone soon.

You need to tell me what the fuck is going on, I said.

Yes, you're right. I do need to tell you. You didn't sign up for any of this.

She took the end of the joint from me again and lit it.

My cancer is back. MY cancer. It's mine. I made it inside me and then they cut it off and poisoned it and it went away but then

I made some more.

I didn't say anything. My heart was hammering in my ears again, and my hands were shaking. Pulling out my tobacco, I made a cigarette, lit it, and handed it to her, suddenly understanding her recent U-turn on smoking. I took the finished joint and dropped it in the ashtray. I refilled her wine glass and passed it to her, took her gently by the shoulders and turned her tiny, folded body on the sofa so that her back was to me. I pulled her against me. She leaned back against my chest and closed her eyes. I could feel her frame vibrating slightly against me as if she was a baby bird I'd found by the roadside. Perhaps I could keep her safe in a cardboard box, and nurse her back to health.

12.

It turned out that I'd ordered us a feast. It arrived over an hour later. The poet had fallen asleep against me, so when I heard the door, I eased myself from underneath her. She barely stirred. I couldn't believe how little she weighed. She was sinew and feathers and down and air. The man at the door handed me two bags bursting with food.

I give her extra, always, he said, and winked at me jovially. She need to eat more. Too small.

I can't argue with that, I said.

I tried to think of a conversation to start with him, to try and calm my brain before going back to her, but I couldn't, and the man clearly needed to leave. If only I could find something meaningful to say, something to draw this stranger into a fleeting friendship. But I could think of nothing. I thanked him and went back inside.

In the poet's kitchen I found a large wooden board to lay out all the aluminium dishes with their little cardboard lids. I took plates and cutlery, and discovered she had chopsticks, which I added to my load. I poured us two more large glasses of the filtered water from her obnoxious fridge. She looked as though she was still sleeping when I went back in, so I carefully laid everything out on the table, and as an afterthought, decided to remove the wine. I put her full glass in the fridge and when I got back in the conservatory, she was awake and snapping the chopsticks between her fingers like a crab.

I'm sorry, she said.

Please don't be. You'll make me uncomfortable.

That's what'll make you uncomfortable? After my little performance?

I don't care about that. Everyone gets drunk sometimes.

You used to make me feel desirable, she said. She was sat primly on the edge of the sofa, that thin spine of hers was perfectly straight.

But I don't anymore?

I can't feel desirable now. I'm defective.

You're magnificent. I still want to fuck you when you're sloppy drunk. And you don't even have a cock. That's saying something.

The poet looked delighted. She didn't say anything in return, but she began to eat as if she'd been starving for days. Of course she used her chopsticks perfectly. She slurped up noodles without getting a spot on her white linen dress.

Do you want to talk about it? I asked.

No. There's not really anything much to talk about. I might not die, if that's what you're wondering. I have a small tumour in my armpit, and they found cancerous cells in the 'excavation site' of my mastectomy. What a fucking thing to call it. I am not archaeology. My tits aren't that old. Or weren't, anyway.

So, what happens now?

No fucking about. She picked up the plastic pot of hot-and-sour soup and sipped it like tea. Surgery next week. They cut it all out, then more chemo. I'm not so worried about the surgery, this time around. It's the bastard chemo that frightens me. I was so tired. So sick. I couldn't fucking write.

You swear a lot when you're drunk.

I swear a lot when I'm cross. Which is what I am, I think. Boiling fucking mad.

I dug into my own noodles. They were delicious. The room smelled of sharp knives.

I used to live in Thailand, you know.

Is that why you're so good with chopsticks?

They eat a lot with their hands in Thailand. Or with a spoon or fork. But I like to eat noodles with chopsticks. It's satisfying.

I want to eat you with my hands.

Maybe I'll let you, she said, and went back to her noodles like a starving child.

13.

The next morning I woke up on the conservatory sofa feeling sticky and confused. The poet was nowhere to be seen, and all the mess from our dinner had been cleared away. My shirt was clinging to my back, and I felt like I was photosynthesising along with all her plants. I was converting the light of her big, white house into energy. I could smell coffee. When I sat up, I realised I'd taken my contacts out the night before. The poet's glass house was blurry.

I remembered that we'd been drinking rum and smoking more of her weed, and that she'd been playing me some of her favourite vinyl and for once that hadn't made me feel like a terrible shit for betraying Michael, even though I knew I wasn't supposed to feel that way, that this was our new way of doing things. She had a first edition of *The Velvet Underground & Nico* and I remembered that she'd played Sunday Morning at least three times while swaying from side to side and smoking my cigarettes, which I'd rolled for her compulsively all night. I'd been afraid that she'd scratch it, but when I said as much, she looked at me with such venom that I didn't mention it again. That morning the vinyl was carefully packed away in its sleeve and back on its shelf out of the sunlight.

When I stood and went into the kitchen the poet was standing at the counter beside a full cafetière. I couldn't see her facial expression with my blurry eyes. She looked like an angel or a ghost. She looked like someone dressed as a ghost for Halloween.

Good morning, she said. She was so composed. It was as if nothing had happened.

That coffee smells excellent.

It's my own blend. She poured me a cup.

There's a towel and a spare toothbrush for you in the downstairs bathroom.

Thank you.

Why were we being so formal? Perhaps she was embarrassed. I didn't want her to be. The closer I got the more I idolised her. I drank my coffee in silence while she read the paper on her iPad. Then I went to the bathroom and showered. Her shower gel was scented with jasmine and vanilla. I'd been right about the jasmine part. And now I smelled like her and not Michael.

When I stepped out of the bathroom and back into the kitchen I hadn't dressed, I just wrapped a towel around my waist. I'd put my contacts in, so now I could focus on her face. She didn't look so composed after all. I went to her, and I kissed her, and she kissed me back and it was completely obvious to us both in that moment what was about to happen.

We stumbled as one to the living room and she drew the curtains to shut out the morning. When we collapsed onto the sofa like awkward teenagers, I realised that's sort of what I was, in this context. I thought about opposites and what they really meant and how she was opposite to me in every way, including how she moved, how she ground her hips into mine. She wasn't ashamed of her scars, which, for some foolish reason, I'd imagined she might be. She held her arms above her head and closed her eyes. She was just as magnificent as I'd told her she was, and I told her again and pressed my face against the puckered skin of her chest and she cradled my head there, as we swayed together as one. She was quivering again like an injured bird, and I realised that for the first time I couldn't put a name to how she smelled.

14.

A few days later I received a call from Ishia. She informed me that the private healthcare team had visited Hetty, and that she had consented to the surgery. I don't know what they said, but my guess would be that they appeared expensive. She has always responded more to money than to people.

Michael thought that we should go and see her again before she was admitted. I told him that all she wanted was the use of his healthcare. It was going to cost him around four thousand pounds. It seemed an obscene amount, especially when they were just cutting a limb off. It wasn't like they were giving her a new one. I wanted to scream at him, to yelp through childish tears that she hated him, that he disgusted her in a way that even I couldn't. The hatred she felt for me was something special, something she cultivated with care, something she raised just as she'd raised me. She loved to hate me. She didn't quite hate Michael, that was the wrong word. She felt contempt for him. When he took her hand and tried to comfort her all she could see was his hands on my body. She didn't want him to touch her. She thought he was dirty.

I didn't shout all this at him, of course. What would be the point? It would just hurt him more, more than that word she called him, a word that he'd already attempted to rationalise since we'd seen her.

Why are you paying for it, I asked him, despite knowing what he'd say. She's not your family, she's barely mine.

I'm paying because it's the right thing to do. And I have plenty of money, why wouldn't I? Besides, you are my family, and she's yours. I know you don't want that to be the case but it is.

She won't be grateful.

I know.

She won't thank you.

She's getting forgetful, you know. She doesn't know what she's saying.

Michael looked at me intently.

This is what happens when people get older. You didn't see it with your dad, but I did with mine. She'll say all sorts of things she doesn't mean.

You're wrong, I replied, but couldn't bring myself to explain why.

He sucked his teeth at me, clicking like a disappointed aunt.

It's her generation, he said. *Things have changed,* he said.

The truth was that every single one of us in that room knew the gravity of that word when she said it, but nobody more than Hetty. That was why she'd chosen to use it.

We didn't go back to the home before her surgery. Michael had a call with her team of doctors, to calm his worries. It seemed that the operation was all rather straightforward. Hetty was a little on the older side, so the general anaesthetic was a slight concern, but it should all be over quick enough, and she would have the very best of care. The best that money could buy. Michael wrote down the date and time of the surgery in his unintelligible handwriting, but I was able to read it well enough to discover that it was the same day as the poet was due to be admitted to hospital.

The poet was going to have her operation at the city hospital, through the NHS, despite her enormous house and the trappings that went with it. She confessed to me that after her problematic relationship with her previous oncologist, she'd briefly gone private, but felt so terribly guilty about it that she'd switched back. Luckily, during the brief window of indulgence (her phrasing), she'd found a doctor she actually liked. A woman this time, and one she was fairly sure wasn't a sociopath, as so many surgeons are (again, her words). This woman had a private clinic but mostly worked for the NHS. She had reprimanded her consultant for using the phrase 'excavation site' and that action alone was enough, apparently, for the poet to decide to trust her with her life. I couldn't see why this mattered so much, but then, I didn't need to.

I learned all this because we had begun to talk on the phone. The poet called me every morning that week, on her early walks. It had been a surprise, at first, when she rang me that early, but it was when Michael was at the gym, and the following morning I woke early again with a start, as if I was late for a meeting. I liked to hear her breathlessness as she climbed the hill, from which she could see the solar panels on the roof of her big, white house.

The day before the surgeries, I went into town. I had a couple of hours of work to do at the shared office, and I wanted to buy a gift for the poet. I realised while staring out of the train window that I was completely terrified. I walked straight to the gym, changed quickly, and ran on the treadmill until I could breathe no more. I needed to find a reason for my heart to beat so fast. A reason that wasn't my rapidly building fear. I was later than I'd planned, getting to the office, and I completed my work in a daze, drinking too much coffee. What does one buy for someone having a tumour removed? Everything I picked up seemed ridiculous. I also realised that the poet already owned everything she could possibly want or need. She had two huge, white properties to fill with old records that I couldn't afford, photographs with famous people and paintings of birds on the walls. I hadn't spotted the arctic tern that I'd bought for her anywhere while I'd been at her house, but then, I hadn't even ventured upstairs. She'd kept me firmly on the ground. I gave up on my shopping trip and went and sat on our bench by the river.

I found myself dialling the number for Hetty's care home. I gave her room number to the receptionist and waited to be put through.

Yes?

It's me.

Yes.

I was calling to wish you good luck for tomorrow.

Yes, well. I suppose I'll see you there after? And *him?*

Michael has taken the day off work to be there when you wake up. You should really thank him; he's paying a fortune for this.

You want me to thank him for having my foot cut off?

Yes, I suppose I do. And I want you to apologise for calling him that horrible thing.

I don't apologise.

It's a disgusting word Hetty.

I've nothing to be sorry for. He is a fag. It's appropriate.

It's exactly the sort of word I'd expect you to use, actually. And, to be clear, I won't be there when you come around tomorrow. I have other commitments.

My heart was hammering again. Perhaps I needed to see a doctor. I heard her sniff down the phone. She was surprised, I could tell.

Sometimes I wonder what I did to deserve a son like you, she said. And you can tell that fag that I don't want him there either.

I hung up the phone.

I'd inherited all my worst qualities from Hetty. But I was beginning to realise that I didn't have to keep them. I rolled a cigarette and watched a mother and son feeding the ducks.

When I got home that afternoon I discovered Michael was already there. He greeted me with a hug when I came through the door. I buried myself in his shoulder. I didn't want to have to tell him about the phone call, about how relentlessly horrible she was, about what she'd said about him. Michael cradled me against him, and I felt the strength of his shoulders under my hands.

I'm frightened, I said into his neck.

I know, he said.

I don't want her to die. I love her.

I know you do.

I've only just found her, and I don't know what I'll do if I lose her, I said into his shoulder.

Shhh, he said. I'm not sure that he heard me.

Michael made me a cup of herbal tea and offered to cook dinner. The lamp in the corner cast a gentle, yellow light across the room, and I remembered when we'd bought it together, at the antiques market down the road from our flat. It was only a few months ago, but everything was so different now. I watched his back as he fiddled with linking his phone to our small speaker. I wasn't sure I could handle any music – I was certain it would just bring more tears. But he put on the radio, and the afternoon play on Radio 4 spilled into the room. I had no idea what it was, and, as always, I found that only hearing the actor's voices made the whole thing feel contrived and overacted. I need to see faces to feel things. But it calmed me down. I wiped my face and took some deep breaths, let the vapor from my tea steam up my glasses. I preferred the world a little steamed up, I thought. Michael began chopping vegetables. I could feel my heartrate decrease.

After dinner, Michael settled on the sofa in front of the TV. There was football on, England were playing, or he probably wouldn't have bothered. I opened my laptop at the table. I'd had an idea for a gift. I spent a few minutes on YouTube, watching instructional videos. I found a sheet of newspaper I wanted to use – containing an article about the poet's new book. I tried to follow the lines and folds made by the peppy American girl in the video, but I couldn't get it right. Occasionally I noticed Michael glance at me from the sofa, but it wasn't until I slammed the scissors down that he came over. He has always been more patient than I am.

Michael leaned over my chair from behind and took the sheet of newspaper from me. His hairless cheek brushed mine. After studying the video for a moment he carried it through to the table in his study, which was covered with pieces of model aeroplanes, scraps of paper, small tubes of glue. I trailed after him, unable to say anything. My fingertips were stained black from the ink. He smelled like mint, like rain, like early mornings. His long, deft fingers began to fold the newspaper. He used a plastic tool to smooth down his confident folds. When he was done, he simply kissed me on my crown and went back to the sofa. It was perfect. A perfect origami swan.

I woke early the next morning, with no call from the poet and with Michael in the bed next to me. I eased myself out of the sheets without waking him and went to make the tea. It appeared we'd switched roles for the day. As the kettle boiled, I texted her to say good morning, and that I'd meet her at the hospital, if she was happy for me to be there. I'd mentioned it a couple of times before, but she hadn't quite said yes or no.

L is driving me, the reply said. I'll be there from 9.30, it would be good to see you. There was just one kiss at the end of the message. I took Michael his tea.

Can I take the car? I asked, as he sat up to take it.

Good morning to you too.

Sorry.

Don't be. Take the car. I'm still going to Hetty.

I know. Don't let her upset you. She's like a wounded bear.

I won't. Don't let her upset you either. You're not like her. You know that don't you?

I didn't. I took his hand.

I love you, he said. He'd not said that for a while.

I love you too Michael.

I didn't have time to drink my tea. I showered quickly and left.

The hospital car park was busy and confusing and expensive, but I managed to arrive in time. The corridors echoed with half-heard snatches of conversation. Titbits about stranger's treatment plans, words like 'outlook' and 'schedule' and 'promising' flitting into my ears as I sat on the blue nylon chair in the waiting area. Follow the blue arrows to the blue waiting area. When I was allowed in to see the poet, she was already wearing a hospital gown and sitting on the bed of a small private room. Her friend, Laurel, sat on the chair next to her, meaning that I had to hover awkwardly in the corner.

I wasn't sure what to do with my arms, so I folded them, but then that seemed severe, so I let them hang beside me.

Laurel, this is the young friend I told you about.

Laurel Willow – she held out a hand for me to shake. I tried not to laugh at her name, but I could tell I had a smirk on my face by the way she looked at me. Seems her parents liked trees. She had grey hair and lines on her face that suggested she usually smiled a lot. She was not smiling at me.

Pleased to meet you, I said. You come here often?

Both women just looked at me. Not a time for jokes. Fair enough.

Laurel turned to the poet. I'm going to get a coffee; would you like anything?

Nil by mouth, said the poet, and made a sign with her hand, like slitting her throat.

Won't be long, said Laurel.

She didn't ask me if I wanted anything. I took her chair once she'd left the room.

Well, I said.

I wanted to give her the swan, but something made me stop myself. It seemed such a stupid, insignificant thing, now we were here. Now she was about to be cut open again.

Well.

How are you feeling?

Cold. Tired.

Can I get you anything?

No.

...

Why are you here? The poet tilted her head to one side as she asked me. She didn't seem angry or sad. I couldn't read her face.

I don't know. I just am.

I'm glad that you are. It doesn't matter why.

She looked terribly pale. All of the women in my life are missing parts. I took her hands and she pulled one of them to her mouth and kissed it.

I want you to touch me, she said.

What? I thought I'd heard wrong. She pushed my hands beneath the starched bedsheets. Here? You can't be serious?

This is my last chance, she said. Touch me.

I was panicking, I didn't know how to respond. She was vulnerable, but not in a way that made me feel powerful, not in a way that could turn me on. She was vulnerable in a way that made me feel helpless, insignificant. Powerless. In a way that could engulf me. I didn't know how to say no to her.

I can't, I said.

She took my hands out of the bedsheets and pressed them to her face.

I'm sorry, she said. That wasn't fair.

That's okay, I said. I can kiss you instead. I kissed her long and hard and I could tell that I was going to cry, except that I couldn't, it would be horrible if I did because I didn't get to feel things today. It was like a terrible birthday, and she was the only one that could cry. We only stopped when we heard Laurel open the door, but she'd clearly seen what was happening.

The three of us weren't forced into awkward silence for too long, because then two nurses began to come in and out, giving an air of perfect efficiency, bustling, and chatting. The poet kept making these awful jokes about how old hat she was at all this. She knew how this worked; she knew what was coming. One of the nurses, the younger one, looked as if she might cry too and I think that was because she knew what was coming as well. But the nurse couldn't cry for the same reason that I couldn't, and not long after that, they wheeled her away.

15.

Hetty was sat upright in the bed. Someone had given her lipstick, it seemed, because she was wearing some and her hair had been curled. Or perhaps it just looked like that before she went in and had stayed exactly where it was like she was a doll. I wouldn't know, this was the first time I'd seen her since she called Michael that nasty word. It had been six days since her operation. There'd been some minor worries about blood clots and the levels of something-or-other, Michael had told me, so she was still here, rather than back at the home being mildly racist. I'm sure she was being racist here too, of course.

It's you, she said.

Yes, I said.

I didn't want to be there. I mean, that much is obvious. I was still trying to understand it myself – why it was that I had taken the car and driven out of town to the private health centre. Michael had been every day since she'd been admitted. I had been in town, spending all my money in the public hospital car park. The car park for the private clinic was free. There was even a water feature. Michael hadn't asked me where I'd been once, nor had he complained once. Hetty had been almost pleasant, he'd told me. Back to their previous tenuous alliance, as if nothing had happened. I did not know why I was here or what I hoped to achieve by it, but here I was.

How are you feeling?

I could see her legs underneath the covers, the single lump of a single foot. I wanted to poke her stump, to see if she felt anything. Sometimes I wasn't even sure if she was alive.

Bored. And in pain, of course. You'd think with the cost of this place they'd give me some decent medication. She looked happy. Satisfied.

You know why they won't, I said. She wrinkled her nose at me.

Hetty has a history of prescription drug abuse. Not that she'd ever acknowledge the fact or describe it as such. But that was the case. Opioids. Began with a bad back after having me, and my 'traumatic birth' (which she liked to remind me of regularly, my first infraction against her). Then she kept going. These days, they're careful what they prescribe her. At my request. I did it to spoil her fun. I couldn't care less what she did to her insides. I'm sure they're all rotten anyway. Eventually they'll just have to put her on the compost heap.

Where have you been?

Busy.

Too busy to visit your ailing mother?

Yes. Exactly that busy.

So why have you bothered now?

To tell you that I won't be visiting anymore, and nor will Michael. If you require anything logistically, then the home can contact us. But I don't want you poisoning my life anymore. I've let it go on for too long.

You came to visit me to tell me that you won't be visiting me? That's stupid, even for you. She sniffed and turned to look out of the window. That was my dismissal.

I walked over to the bed and placed the bunch of yellow roses I'd brought onto the table. Rosa Sun Flare, the variety my father had always bought for her. The roses were framed with gypsophila and reminded me of a '70s wedding bouquet. Hetty had them in her wedding bouquet. There used to be a photo on our mantlepiece of her and my father together at the wedding breakfast. He looked directly into the camera with a wide smile. She looked off into the distance. The roses smelled of liquorice. It was the best goodbye I could have hoped for.

After leaving Hetty for what would hopefully be the final time, I drove back to the city hospital. My stomach felt tiny, as if it had been shrunk down to a tight ball of rubber bands. Every time I tried to eat it felt as though I were pushing the food between the strings of rubber. So I hadn't been eating much. Michael wanted me to talk to my doctor about having anxiety, but I thought it was unnecessary. I didn't *have* anxiety; I was just anxious. There's a difference.

The poet's chemotherapy wouldn't begin until six weeks after her surgery. Today she was leaving the hospital, and I was driving her home. I'd stopped at an M&S on the way in and bought us smoothies and a punnet of fresh cherries. They were glistening in the passenger seat next to me as I drove, obscene somehow, wet and red. I was nervous about seeing her, but then I seemed to be nervous about seeing everyone. I was full of adrenaline from my encounter with Hetty, and only realised as I parked that I had not bought the poet any flowers. For a second, I was worried, but I rationalised that she would prefer something sweet and edible. Especially after a week of hospital food. Besides, flowers weren't allowed in NHS hospitals. Only rich people were allowed flowers by their beds. Except that the poet was rich, of course.

When I entered the room, the poet was sat on the edge of the bed wearing a linen summer dress in a dusty blue colour. She had her short hair pulled back from her face and a concentrated expression as she listened to the doctor, who stood by the window next to her. The doctor had those long fake eyelashes that people get glued to their real lashes, and spiky red nails. This confused me, as I was sure that nail varnish wasn't permitted by hospital staff.

Hello, the doctor said, and flashed white teeth at me. I see you've brought some snacks.

I did, I said. Cherries. I sat at the end of the bed.

Excellent. The doctor turned back to the poet. You'll want to be eating lots of fresh foods. Something like cherries is a great place to start, to try and get your appetite back a bit.

Thank you, Marilyn, said the poet. I'll see you in a few days.

You will, and good luck with it all. The doctor left the room without saying anything else to me, or even acknowledging my presence.

Are you ready?

I am. I am extremely ready to go home.

I brought you a gift.

Not just the cherries?

I brought it when you went in for surgery. I meant it to be good luck, or something, but then I didn't give it to you. I'm not sure why. It's a little squashed now from being in my pocket.

I handed her the origami swan. She took it gently and began to smooth the folds in the paper and sharpen the points of its wings.

She's lovely, she said.

She?

Yes, she.

The poet smiled at me and dropped the swan into her bag as if it were her housekeys. I'm not sure what response I was expecting, but that wasn't it.

Shall we go? she said.

She walked smartly to the door with far too much energy for someone who had just had surgery. Why wouldn't she let me look after her?

I met Jessica for dinner. I desperately needed to talk to someone who could see the black and whites of things. I was blinded by grey, everywhere I looked.

You look thin, she said.

Nobody ever says hello to me anymore.

I am thin, I replied.

Good job we are here then. Let me get some meat on those bones and that frown off your face. You're not so pretty when you frown. You're spoiling my view of you.

I didn't say anything. The waitress led us to our table. We'd chosen a Turkish place. I wanted to eat a huge pile of meat. I wanted them to keep bringing me food until I drowned under the weight of it all.

So, tell me, she said, once we had drinks in our hands.

I don't know what to tell. The poet is home from the hospital. She calls me early every morning on her walk. She's not supposed to be walking again yet, but she is.

What do you talk about?

Jessica took the maraschino cherry from her Manhattan with her finger and thumb and rolled it between them before popping it in her mouth. I didn't want to think about cherries, about redness, about the poet, about my origami swan dying quietly in the bottom of the poet's handbag.

We talk about the birds she sees on her walks. We talk about how she wants to get a dog. About how she misses work, and that she's bored.

Do you talk about fucking?

No. We've never talked about it. It just happened. Still happens, when I visit her. But not very often. And I'm not sure I like doing it, now. I don't want to break her.

Jessica snorted. You won't break her, she said. She looked like she wanted to roll her eyes but stopped herself at the last moment. It got my back up.

She's so fragile, Jess. She has hollow bones.

Physically she might be fragile, although not as fragile as you think, I bet. But mentally? She is iron compared to you, my sweet.

In one fluid movement Jess threw back the last of her drink and did that thing at the waiter to get another round.

You, my love, are a delicate little chicken. A fluffy wee bairn.

Fuck you, I said.

No, fuck you. She smiled. You're friends with me because I tell the truth, remember. You are so concerned with where the poet fits into your life that you haven't considered for a second where you fit into hers. Who's using who here, do we think?

Why does someone have to be?

Because they always are. Your poet is stronger than you. Think about it.

Fuck you Jess.

Shall we eat dessert? she said, ignoring me and smiling wickedly. I fancy some baklava and that rice pudding. The waiter brought our drinks over and she ordered one of everything.

The next morning my head was sore from all the drinking with Jess, and my tiny, rubber-band stomach hurt from filling it with food. When I picked up my phone I saw a message from Jess – she was upset, something about this awful man she'd been seeing. I opened the message but didn't respond. Michael was out at the gym, as usual, and the poet was phoning me, as usual. I decided not to take the call. I let it go to voicemail, and a minute or two later I received a text message.

Come over, it said. Today I feel strong, let's go on my walk together?

I wanted to reply saying that I wasn't her puppy to take walking, that she couldn't just summon me whenever she fancied it. Clearly Jess had got under my skin. But as my thumb wavered over the screen of my phone, I realised that's exactly what I was. I was the juvenile, the student, the subordinate. When she said jump, I was already in the air, licking at her fingers for crumbs. The other thing that I realised, in that moment, was that I liked it.

16.

The air was cool. It was still before 8am, and although the light screamed full day into my eyes, something about the texture of the air hinted at the approaching season change. Soon all the green would turn to yellow, to orange, and finally to brown, when it would wither and die. I wondered where we would be then. Would I ever walk with the poet when she was dressed in a warm coat, or was I forever going to see her in the array of expensive linen summer dresses she favoured, flowing and light? Would we ever walk by frozen water, stand together under trees gripped by frost?

I was wearing jeans, which I was glad of, but something about my shoes and socks felt restrictive, so I kicked them off and stood on the grass in my bare feet. It was slightly damp, and I'd expected it to feel cool, but it didn't. The earth radiated warmth, as if it knew it was still summer, as if it was trying to tell me the very same thing. That it wasn't over yet. The warmth wasn't over. The poet locked the front door to her big white house and when she saw my feet she laughed.

Don't you want to put your shoes inside or something? she asked.

No, they can stay there.

You'll get muddy.

I know, I want to.

We walked up the grassy hill at the back of her house in silence. She was wearing a linen dress, as I'd known she would be. She had a knitted shawl wrapped around her shoulders, or perhaps it was a blanket, it was hard to tell. She wore leather sandals. The slope was steep, but smooth, and the poet didn't tire at first, even of me incessantly asking if she was okay, if she needed to rest. Eventually she rounded on me.

I'll need to rest when the chemo starts. If I rest now, I'll die. I can't waste any time.

The words sounded round and soft in her mouth, like the inside of a fresh loaf of bread. Then she turned, and kept walking, and I stopped asking if she was okay.

I could see her yellowhammer tattoo when she lifted her dress away from the ground, so it didn't get damp from the dew. The sandy earth was sticking to my feet. We walked in silence again, and the path twisted off into the woods. It had been raining, hard, and the undergrowth was so lush and wet that I could hear it growing, hear it twitching and seething as it sucked in the moisture and energy and turned it into green. I kept thinking about stories, about love stories and lust stories, good ones. About TV and film that I'd seen that I actually cared about, that had managed to impact on me (which didn't happen often, because I prefer to live inside books). You don't often see the in-between, do you? You don't often see the part where you walk in silence and don't touch one another, the part where the shards from an explosion float to the ground, and you have to get up again the next day. The part where you put the washing on and go to work and pretend everything is fine and all the while your chest is heaving from your invisible wounds. You see the chasms of heartbreak, the wet cheeks and dramatic sobs and hard goodbyes, but you don't see the agonised conversations with friends, the fabrications of a narrative that doesn't show us in our horrible, fractured, human light. Perhaps I loved the poet and I loved Michael. Perhaps I didn't love either of them.

The path wound upward, and a small stream fell away beneath us to one side. The higher we climbed, the further the water had to fall, and the louder it became. I could hear the water and I could hear the birds chattering and I could feel insects moving around me. I felt lonely and lost and I felt like I didn't know who or what I was anymore. I was a man walking in the woods with a woman who I might love, or might not feel anything for. I wanted to be her, to be like her, to have her success and to know the people she knew. But it wasn't just that. I wanted to be around her and breathe in her energy just as I was now breathing the energy of those woods, of the falling water and the pulsating greenery around me. I hadn't felt like this in a long time. I needed to write something, before I did myself some real damage.

The path veered out of the woods, and into a clear, grassy area. My feet were caked with mud, and I wiped them on the damp grass. The sun was beginning to warm up again. It was going to be a hot day; I could feel it.

It's lovely, isn't it, said the poet.
It is.
I'm frightened about the next stage, she said.
I know you are. I am too.
Frightened for me or for you?
Both.

17.

I stayed at the poet's house all day and all night. I texted Michael, and invented something about going to the theatre with Jess, but I don't know why, I could've told him where I was. He was with Nicolás anyway. He was happy. I think perhaps I didn't tell him where I was because then it would exist in the real world. My time with her belonged to me alone, it did not belong to a world with Michael in it, or rent and bills and work and washing. I would not let our time together cross over into my life with Michael and his life with Nicolás. Keeping it this way made me feel as though I had agency.

After our walk, the poet and I decided to make a picnic and take it back up through the woods, to the clearing from which we could see her house. The sun was strong, and I was concerned about burning. The poet found me some factor 50 sun cream in her downstairs bathroom, that had clearly been there for a long time. It was a roll-on designed for children, and the cream was blue until you rubbed it in. It made me wonder what part of the poet's life contained children who needed blue sun cream. I rubbed in the blue cream and inhaled the smells of artificial coconut and honey, the smells of holidays and swimming in the sea. I wished I could swim in the sea.

The poet told me to make what I could out of the contents of her fridge, while she showered and dressed. I'd thought she had already showered and dressed, but I didn't mind, as I liked the idea of spending time in her house without her eyes on me. The way she said it made it sound as if there would be nothing in her fridge, but

I found fat juicy grapes, brie wrapped in wax paper, fresh rocket. There was rye bread in the breadbin and eggs in a small basket by one of the huge windows.

I made sandwiches, and hardboiled the eggs as a snack. I packed us an apple each, and three tangerines. The poet had matching Tupperware in her cupboard. I made a pot of her special coffee and poured some into a flask. I poured myself a cup. The poet had not yet come downstairs, and I could hear a hairdryer. I took my coffee into the conservatory and sat on the sofa. I stared at the photo of the poet and Salman Rushdie as I'd wished to do the first night we were here. There were some wooden chopsticks on the table, a physical reminder of our first night together, and I wondered whether that meant the poet cared about me or whether she just ate a lot of Thai food.

I realised my muddy feet had made marks on her cream rug, and I was in the process of cleaning up when the poet came downstairs. She was wearing denim shorts and a white shirt, with the leather sandals of that morning. She looked amused as she stared down at me with the sweeping brush in my hand, and I realised she often looked amused when she looked at me. I didn't like how that felt.

Shall we go? she said.

We ate our sandwiches in the baking sunshine in the clearing at the top of the hill. The clouds were strung along the horizon like fairy lights on a garden fence. The poet rubbed some of the blue sun cream into her arms and cheeks, so that we both smelled like plastic coconuts and synthetic bees. We were as hungry as we'd have been if we'd been walking for hours, when truthfully it wasn't that far. The sun had dried the dew from the grass, and my bare feet were caked with dusty mud. I rolled up the cuffs of my jeans and debated for a moment taking off my shirt. But that felt too intimate.

I have always been described as beautiful. Or sometimes pretty, which is worse. It started when I was a child, and my teachers would admire my pale blonde hair. But then it darkened and is now a muddy brown. Muddy like my feet. I don't think boys are meant to be beautiful. They don't know what to do with it. I certainly didn't. When I look at beautiful women, especially young ones, there is a resignation to them. They understand that they have been gifted a very particular currency. They have lots of it to spend but it's laced with mercury, or perhaps lead. Some kind of metal that will eventually make them sick. I do not desire young women. I rarely desire any women at all, but young women make me sad. Along with the resignation that young women possess, comes a certain amount of understanding. They know what to do with their beauty. I never did. I worried that my face was too feminine, that my full lips would somehow give me away, would let the straight boys at school know that I wanted to taste them. And I wasn't wrong, most of the time.

Now that I'm older, I'm careful to dress in a masculine way. I never shave my face cleanly. But when people talk about my beauty it still makes me panic. I could not take off my shirt in front of the poet because she might read some meaning into it that I hadn't intended. Despite having seen me naked, multiple times, the idea of being shirtless and barefoot and lying on the grass in front of the poet made me feel as if I had no skin, and that my flesh was just open to the sun.

After our picnic the poet walked me further, to the nearby village that spilled across the top of the hill. It was muggy and hot, and we were both sweating. The poet had caught the sun, even while wearing blue sun cream, and she had a little stripe of red across her cheeks. I liked how it looked, and kissed her, right there in the street where people could see us. It made her jump.

She took me to the ruins of a churchyard. There was an ice cream van by the gates selling proper ice creams, not the stuff out of the machine. I don't like Mr Whippy, it smells like aluminium. I bought us a mint chocolate chip cone each and we took them into the churchyard. The gravestones were all crammed together and pushed upward from beneath by the roots of the sycamore trees. It reminded me of the Thomas Hardy tree at St Pancras Old Church in London and for a moment I wanted to weep over how many skeletons there were underneath our feet.

We looked at all the graves and said the names aloud and invented character profiles for each of them. The ice cream was melting in the sun, and we had to eat it quickly. Now we smelled like honey and coconuts and swimming in the sea and mint chocolate chip ice cream. The poet kept listing all the plans she had for the next couple of weeks, all the galleries and museums she would take me to, all the books she wanted to read and films she would see and concerts she would attend. I realised then that she thought she was going to die.

18.

While we sat in the sun the poet told me the story of what she described as the most beautiful moment of her life. She had attended a talk given by her favourite author when she was eighteen years old (before I was born, she said, which was incorrect, but I didn't mention it). She had clasped two books by this author to her chest, one she'd bought for herself, but the other had been lent to her by her friend's mother. This woman, the mother, had introduced the poet to the joys of books, of writing, and most especially to the poet's favourite author.

At the end of the talk there was a queue to have your book signed. The poet was at the talk with said friend, who volunteered erudite questions during the talk, and who shook the author's hand boldly when they reached the front of the queue. When the poet got her books signed, she'd wanted to get the one that belonged to the mother dedicated to her. But she was so awestruck that she'd only managed to say her own name, which meant that both books were addressed to her, not to the mother. She was embarrassed, for a moment, but afterwards she realised it was because she'd been having a religious experience. Her friend had loved the author with a professional admiration, with an awe for her talent. But the poet had been in the presence of Her New God. When she'd got home that night, she'd phoned the friend's mother and apologised for getting the wrong name in the book. The mother, Anna, replied that she wasn't to worry, because it had always been her book – she'd just been waiting to find the real owner so she could give it to her. The poet thought it was the kindest anyone had ever been. Anna died of breast cancer a few years later, she told me.

Perhaps that's why I'm so frightened, she said.

Our hands were sticky from the ice cream and from the sun cream, but we were still hungry, so we ate a tangerine each and sat quietly looking at the graves and thinking about her story.

19.

That night I slept in the poet's bed for the first time. She had an ensuite bathroom, and I discovered that the painting of the arctic tern was hanging above her toilet. I couldn't decide how to feel about that, but eventually settled on the conclusion that it was a good thing. It meant that she liked the painting, at least. I couldn't see the origami swan anywhere.

The poet had linen bedsheets to match her linen summer dresses. They were the colour of evergreen trees. Her bed was wide like a hotel bed, and high off the floor. It dwarfed her. When we fucked I held her arms above her head and they disappeared into the bedsheets as if she'd plunged them into water. She bit me on the neck and there was a mark there the next day. We were both sunburned and tired from our walk, and still smelled like sun cream. I wanted to shower but I hadn't the energy. The poet did shower because she had to keep the area around her dressings clean. Since she'd had the surgery, she kept a camisole on when we were fucking. It made me sad, because her lack of shame around her scars was deeply attractive to me. Here was a woman who was not afraid of being exactly herself. I wondered if I would one day be brave enough to be exactly myself, and to fight death for the second time in just a few short years. You are not supposed to use the language of battle when you describe cancer anymore, she'd told me. It's now seen as problematic, as it implies there are worthy winners and losers. I could understand the logic, but I believed she was fighting none the less. She was fighting to hold onto every scrap that she had; she would go down in a heady haze of books and culture and music and as many orgasms as I could give her, which I was actually getting quite good at. I had always understood that it was meant to be difficult to pleasure a woman, but as far as I could tell from my limited experience, it was like surfing. Just follow the tides. Let the sea tell you where to go and what to do. Follow the tides and don't stop.

The next morning the poet woke before the sun, saying that she needed to write. She practically threw me out of the door to her big, white house, but before she did, she lent me a book by her favourite author. When I opened it, I saw that the poet's favourite author had written the word JOY! inside, and the poet's first name in cursive handwriting.

This is how he sleeps,
perfectly quiet like entering a blackbird's eye.

Miruna Fulgeanu

20.

When I arrived home that day, Michael was sat at his desk drinking black coffee and looking at paperwork. It was another hot day, and he wasn't wearing a shirt. I leaned down and pressed my face into the top of his head. I read some of the words on the screen.

Contracts?

The new gym. It's all going through. Building work should start next week, hopefully.

Excellent. You're going to take over the world.

We are.

Not sure what I've got to do with it.

You're my trophy wife.

There's a reason why women don't like that phrase, you know.

Trophy husband then.

Not the bit I meant. I don't want to be a trophy.

Do you want to be a husband?

Oh ha ha.

I'm not laughing.

I looked at his husky-blue eyes. He wasn't joking. I'm not sure he was asking me anything, either, but he looked at me with such an open, inviting stare. I couldn't tell you what it was that I felt in that moment, except that I knew I wanted to smell mint every morning. It looked like Jessica was right about everything. I'd have to be careful not to tell her, she was already unbearable most of the time anyway.

I didn't respond verbally, but I wrapped myself around his neck, and stayed there, leaning my face into him. He continued with his work, totally calm, as if he hadn't just said what he'd said.

Eventually, it became clear that he couldn't type properly with me draped over him like a shawl, so I kissed him and left him to it. I showered the scent of the poet from my skin with scalding hot water, and I used his shower gel again. It seemed only appropriate that I took on his smell while I was at home with him. When I looked in the mirror, I saw that I'd caught the sun too, and my normally pale face looked almost ruddy. I felt like I was wearing the skin of a dead lamb, nuzzling thirstily at the teat of my life with Michael. It seemed he loved me anyway, despite my obvious and macabre disguise.

I took the car to be washed. I felt like I was cleaning all the parts to my life, as if I was about to sell them. To put them up for auction to the highest bidder. The two men washing the car must have been in their fifties. Dark skin, strong arms. They washed it as though it were a baby, gently lifting the wipers to clean beneath them, opening the doors and the boot and tenderly taking out the contents and laying them out on a bench with reverence. There was a binbag in the boot that we used to put our dirty shoes on, and the man from the car wash shook it out and carefully folded it into a square. It made me think of Michael's strong hands folding the origami swan, and I knew if I watched them any longer, I would cry again. I really had to stop this crying business. I signalled to the men that I'd come back and collect the car when they were done. They smiled back benignly and waved. This was how they spent their days, every day. Trying to be the best at what they did. What I did, supposedly, was write, and yet I'd not written for so long it was beginning to give me a stomach-ache.

I walked to the park. There was a group of teenagers sat underneath a tree in a circle. They drank cider and played tinny music on their phones; music that had been written before they were born. They all wore baggy jeans and black t-shirts, had kohl rubbed under their eyes and various piercings. I wondered whether they would believe me if I told them I used to be like them. *I'm a creep, I'm a weirdo.* I am definitely still both of those things, perhaps especially now, while wearing designer jeans and conforming to the new group I belonged to. Butterflies passed me by to land on a nearby buddleia bush. A fat man was walking a tiny puppy. It was so overwhelmed by being outside and in the world that it kept tripping and couldn't decide whether to bound ahead of his owner or walk safely behind him.

Michael text me and told me to wear something pretty later, as he was going to take me out. He put an emoji of a woman in a dress dancing. I hated how he spoke to me sometimes. I hated the thought of us conforming to some stereotype, whilst simultaneously knowing that we did. I immediately began looking for job ads on my phone. I could hardly complain about our dynamic while also letting him pay for my life. Michael calls me pretty a lot. Or sometimes beautiful. The poet never calls me beautiful. In fact, I don't remember her ever referring to my appearance.

Despite my initial irritation at Michael's message, I did dress myself well that night. I'd bought new cologne, a musky, cinnamon scent, and I doused myself. Perhaps I could have a scent of my very own and did not need to take on the smells of those around me like some kind of chameleon. I put on my favourite jeans; expensive, well cut, flattering to my long form. I wore a crisp white shirt that set off my new tan. I trimmed my beard down to designer stubble. I put some oil through my hair, which was longer than it had been in a while. If my mother could have seen me, she'd have been violently ill. I stared at myself in the mirror. I was beautiful. It was okay for me to think that about myself, as long as other people didn't say it. I went as far as putting lip balm on, adding a sheen to my full lips. The lips that I now made a habit of pressing to two different skins: one tanned and taut, one freckled and pale.

I heard a car horn beeping and looked out of the window to discover it was Michael. He waved at me excitedly. I looked in the mirror once more and pushed my hair back out of my face.

My fingers were long, moisturised, my nails clean. My eyes are so brown now they are almost black. Not so muddy, anymore. They are beginning to look like my father's eyes. Like the falcon's eyes.

We ate dinner at an expensive fish restaurant in the city centre. Michael was iridescent, as he always is when there is a large amount of money coming his way. He flirted and joked with everyone that came anywhere near us. He's so handsome, and I could see it reflected in the eyes of everyone he spoke to, like he donated some of his beauty to them by engaging them in conversation. They all stared at his husky eyes and couldn't pull away. Michael and I know the owners of the restaurant personally. The chef: older, grey, svelte. His partner: ex-model, attractive, stupid, but with excellent taste. The building used to be a bank, and the stupid, younger one had done a wonderful job of doing it out. There were hammered gold fittings, blue and green velvet booths, 1920s style glassware. The food cost a fortune, but it was also excellent.

I smiled and batted my eyes at those who came to our table to say hello but couldn't muster much of the kinetic social energy that emanated from Michael. I had the monkfish, in a cream sauce. It was chewy like meat, yet slippery and salty. Michael began to talk faster and got up to use the bathroom repeatedly. He was drinking Italian lager in those tall, narrow pint glasses that always look like they're going to fall over. He was drinking them like water. I sipped my Negroni slowly. Michael went into the kitchen to thank the chef. It wasn't an open kitchen, but my mind's eye bored a hole through the wall and watched them chop cocaine with an expensive kitchen knife, on the stainless-steel counter. What efficient, powdery lines they would be enjoying. I watched the ex-model burst through the swinging kitchen door, to join Michael and the chef. I imagined their hands on Michael, pulling at his expensive suit jacket, undoing the buttons to his shirt. I imagined him skewered between them like the Tasmanian salmon in chilli butter that he'd eaten for his dinner. I couldn't tell if I was turning myself on or just being depressing. Probably the latter. I ordered another Negroni with a flick of the wrist. I'd been learning from Jessica.

When Michael returned to the table, I could see the veins in his temples pulsing. I wanted to press my fingers into them.
Would you like a dessert? he asked.
No, I'm going to have another cocktail. Are you having fun?
I am. Are you?
Yes, I said.
Perhaps it was even true. I really had no idea. I decided to drink my second Negroni much faster than the first.

We stayed at the restaurant until past closing. I could see the irritation in the waiting staff's faces as they finished clearing and setting all the tables but ours. The chef kept putting his hand on my leg. The ex-model kept shooting me looks of disgust. I felt like a statue, or a piece of art. I felt like I had absolutely no agency whatsoever. I felt like my intellect had disappeared from me, like it was floating up into the sky, because it didn't matter here. We were brought more and more drinks, I had a little row of them in front of me, as I doggedly sipped my second Negroni. There was champagne, sambuca with coffee beans floating in it, and Irish coffee. I especially didn't want to drink the Irish coffee, because the last time I'd had one had been with the poet. I wanted to step into that memory, to feel the wooden handle of my golf umbrella and smell the scent of jasmine. To eat simple and delicious pasta. There was a plate of grilled sardines on the table that we'd hardly touched – the chef had sent them over for us to try. All their little faces were staring at me. Nobody offered me any cocaine, but I felt so far removed from all of them that I eventually asked for some.
May I have some cocaine, I said. Like, please may you pass the salt.
Michael laughed at me.
So vulgar, to say it out loud, said the ex-model.

The chef punched him on the arm. Come with me, he said.

I followed him into the kitchen. It was echoey and empty compared to the opulence of the restaurant. It made me think of the hospital. I imagined the poet laid out naked on the stainless-steel counter. I imagined someone cutting into her, continuing to take pieces of her, pieces she didn't have spare to give away. Her cancer was like some terrible poisonnier, filleting her tiny form so that she could be poached in milk, and seasoned with shallots and lemon juice. Soon there would be nothing left. The chef put his hand on the small of my back. He pushed my face down towards the lines he'd chopped on the counter. I snorted two of them, using his £50 note. You can imagine what happened next.

Michael hailed a taxi, and one pulled up immediately like they do in films. He called the taxi with that obnoxious two-fingered whistle that some men use. I've never seen a woman whistle like that. I don't think they feel the need. I don't know how to whistle like that. Maybe it's something fathers are supposed to teach their teenage sons. Michael had paid the bill, but most of our meal was on the house. Rich people don't have to pay for things.

Well, that was fun, he said, once we were inside the car.

Yes, I said.

I've not done that in a while.

No, I said.

I want to show you something.

He was so happy. Why was he so happy? I felt like I'd been sucked dry. I felt like a seed pod drifting away in the wind. Michael read an address from his phone to the taxi driver.

We were driving for about twenty minutes. I allowed my eyes to stop focussing and stared at the streams of light through the window. When we pulled up, it was outside a huge concrete structure in the most recently gentrified area of the city. Michael handed the taxi driver some cash and told him there was more if he'd wait for us. The driver happily agreed.

There was a doorman sitting at a concierge desk in the entranceway to the building. Michael smiled at him confidently and shook his hand.

A pleasure to see you again, sir, said the doorman.

We are just taking a little look, Michael said. Are the elevators operational?

They are, sir.

Excellent.

Are the elevators operational? What an odd-sounding Americanism. My heart was jumping in my chest and my throat was numb. I wanted nothing more than to lie down on the marble floor and wait for this day to be over. Michael gave me a key of cocaine in the elevator. He watched me sniff it in the full-length mirror, his other hand on the back of my head. The elevator took us to the roof. I noticed how my brain had immediately adopted the word elevator, even though I knew it as a lift. I had no agency, and no brain anymore, apparently.

Michael walked me out onto the roof by the hand. I was hit by the most delicious breeze. The moon sat fat and low in the sky, nearly full. A pregnant moon? Is that a phrase? She was tinged with orange. We sat together on a small wall, overlooking the glitter of the city windows. I say sat, but Michael kept jumping up, rabbiting on about how the gym would look when he was done, and what he was going to do with the roof space, and how many more members he could take on. How much more money.

Money, money. I said it aloud a couple of times and it sounded weird, like I'd stopped it from being a word. My mouth was dry, and my brain felt slippery and salty like the monkfish. I wasn't really listening, but I reengaged when I heard him say, again, that we should get married.

21.

Michael is the sort of person who goes for a run to get rid of his hangover. You know the type. He was up before me to drive to the gym and hammer the treadmill for the best part of an hour. He is not the type to run outside. Too messy. When he came back the smell of alcohol oozed from his pores. I woke up to him cooking scrambled eggs. I shuffled into the kitchen and dug around in the freezer for crumpets.

You shouldn't eat those. I've made you some eggs.

Eggs will make me sick.

I toasted the crumpets anyway, but they tasted terrible with the low-fat spread Michael always bought. I did my best to eat them. Michael put a plate of eggs in front of me and I pushed them away. I felt horrific, despite drinking only two cocktails. I watched as Michael studiously ignored his gag reflex and forced the eggs down his throat. His eyes were bloodshot.

I've been thinking, he said.

Uh oh.

Hilarious. I've been thinking that we should get on with the wedding plans pretty quickly. Hetty isn't going to be around forever, and it's important that she be there. I know she'll hate it, but it might also provide her with some peace, to know that you'll always be cared for.

This was the worst hangover I'd ever had.

Right, I said.

I didn't remember Michael actually proposing. And I certainly didn't remember saying yes to anything, although it appeared he'd decided I had. Unsurprising, as he hadn't listened to a single word

I'd said that night.

So, you'll organise it then. I'm obviously too busy with the new gym. It needn't be a huge affair. Something classy. Traditional.

I could feel bile rising in my throat, mixing with the bite of crumpet that I couldn't quite swallow. I couldn't swallow any of it, in fact.

Tell me, Michael, in this fantasy of yours – where my shrivelled cunt of a mother attends our 'traditional' gay wedding – will you be inviting Nicolás?

I walked out and locked myself in the bathroom. I coughed and heaved up the bite of crumpet, sat down on the cool floor and stayed very still. I heard Michael finish his breakfast and leave the flat. He didn't say another word.

Would you like to come for a swim with me?

I opened the text from the poet as I stepped out of the shower. Yes, I replied. No further comment. Yes, your honour, I would like to come for a swim with you, and wash away the explosion of shit that has just rained down on what I thought was my life.

That was easy, she replied. *Meet me at the house. Don't worry about towels, we can take mine.*

When I pulled up at the poet's big, white house, she was already on the doorstep, bouncing on the balls of her feet. When I glanced at my phone and saw the date, I realised it was exactly two weeks until her chemotherapy started. She had a canvas bag on one shoulder, and another on the floor in front of her. She ran over with both and threw them in the back seat, jumping in the front. I hadn't expected this.

Are you ready? she said.

She buckled her seatbelt, but the top part stretched over her neck and away from her armpit and her chest. Away from the pieces that were missing. That couldn't possibly be safe. Her cheeks were pink, and I couldn't help but think how unbelievably healthy she looked. It was hard not to compare her to Michael, and his strict ideas about health that somehow allowed for the odd night of hammering cocaine and strong, terrible lager. I preferred the poet's idea of health, one that included ice cream and fresh fruit and being outdoors.

The poet directed me out of the track to her house, up the hill and past the village, past the gates to the cemetery where she'd told me her stories. The hill just kept going up and up and I was finding it hard to imagine where we would find water on the top of the hill, when she told me to pull over, next to the sign for an alpaca farm.

We're the first ones, she said, with satisfaction.

She handed me one of the canvas bags and set off even further up the hill at a pace. I was sweating and panting, and the sun was already high in the sky. The path levelled off and we walked through a scrubby field housing a few sheep. They looked up at us with indifference and didn't run away. We passed two signs that said Polite Notice: Strictly No Swimming. I enjoyed the wording of them so much that I resolved to write something including that line. I could smell cut grass and gasoline.

We approached a small reservoir, perhaps the size of two swimming pools. The poet threw her belongings to the ground and pulled off her linen dress in one movement. She was naked underneath. To my utter surprise she ran at full pelt, skidded down the stone edge of the water and dived in. It was a messy dive, imperfect, there was a huge splash. I stripped off my clothes. Something about her energy was making me nervous, but it was a good kind of nervous. She had so much life in her tiny form that for just a second, I allowed myself to think that she'd be okay. I didn't jump in dramatically like she did, but instead eased myself down the bank. I was nervous of smashing my toes into the stone edges.

Just jump, she said. It's deep as soon as you're away from the edge.

I don't know how to jump like she does.

I continued my slow descent. There were flickering blue dragonflies gathering at the edge of the water. I could see tiny fish swarming over the stones. I wanted to go slowly, to feel all the sensations. When I was finally submerged, I discovered the water was quite warm.

The poet was a chaotic swimmer. Perhaps unfairly, I'd imagined her falling into a rhythmic breaststroke and keeping her whole head above water. In fact, she swam like a child. Or perhaps an eel. She was all wriggles and splashes, plunging underwater unexpectedly only to surface further away, looking at me impatiently. When I reached out to touch her, I marvelled again at her tiny body, a taut mass of tendon and sinew. Of course, under water she really did weigh nothing, but to me it felt the same as when I lifted her onto her huge, forest bed in her big, white house. We decided to do a lap of the deep middle section. I revelled in the feeling of knowing the bottom was far below me. I wanted to sink down there and sleep on the silty bed. I began to feel the effects of my hangover again, but the poet didn't lose her breath for a second.

Have you been writing? she asked, and then dove under, only to surface again a few feet away and look expectantly at me for an answer.

No, I admitted. I've not written anything properly for weeks. Every time I try, I find myself shaken. Weakened, perhaps.

I took my turn to dive under and swim away, like we were playing some strange relay.

I'm not sure I believe in writer's block, as such. I can feel the words, almost see them, but I can't quite catch them. I'm out of practice or something.

How often do you try?

Not often.

Well, that's your problem, then. The poet floated on her back with her arms out to the sides. Sometimes you just have to be in the room. Get your bum on the seat. If you do that often enough then the words'll fly close enough for you to catch them. She took a deep breath and dropped beneath the surface again. When she came back up, I watched her eyes follow a flicker of red and blue as it dipped across the surface of the water.

Did you see it? she asked.

I did, I said.

You know, the bullet trains in Japan were inspired by a kingfisher. The poet's eyes were dancing all around to catch another glimpse.

They used they used the shape of the beak as a model, to prevent a sonic boom every time the train entered a tunnel.

When she saw a flash of the tiny bird again, she laughed out loud.

We swam for hours. When we finally crawled up the bank my muscles were softened and supple, my fingertips wrinkled. I felt diluted, as if I'd begun to blend in with the water, the fish, the insects, and the birds. We lay on our towels in the sun in silence. The heat was almost oppressive once we were under the sun. I noticed that the poet no longer wore dressings on the wounds from her surgery. They looked neat and clean. She had her arms above her head and the soft hair on her underarms glinted reddish in the sun. I'd always imagined her as a swallow, if she were a bird, but I decided that I was wrong. She was a kingfisher. I rolled a cigarette and lit it, and she held out her hand immediately, without opening her eyes. I gave it to her and made myself another one.

The poet had slathered herself with sun cream, not blue this time, and I noticed that no matter how we moved to catch some shade from the tree, the sun always found her first. The sun was always searching for her. Just as I began to feel so hot that I couldn't bear it anymore, it began to rain. Most of the sky was still blue; the poet still lay bathed in pure summer light, yet fat, heavy raindrops began to thud into the dry grass. I could hear it peppering the water. Swallows danced, dipping down to catch surprised insects. I lay perfectly still, listening, and imagined magical feathered trains breaking the speed of sound.

22.

For the next four days, I barely saw Michael. He was back late and up earlier than ever. Meanwhile, I was sleeping like the dead. Sleeping more than I'd ever slept before. After eating my dinners in our little kitchen, alone, I could barely focus my eyes enough to read a page or two of a book, before stumbling to bed. I'd wake up early, but not early enough to catch sight of Michael. I could tell he'd slept in the bed next to me, and the shower was always steamed up, the trail of breadcrumbs leading me to his marked lack of presence. We hadn't spoken, really, since our row, and as far as I knew he still believed we were engaged. The poet phoned me every morning, on her walk, so I got to hear her breathless voice as she climbed that hill. I felt her voice was getting a little more breathless each time, wavering a little more. She stayed on the phone a little longer each time too, before disappearing to make her expensive coffee and to write. She was more of a writer than I would ever be.

Four days of the same routine, of me filling the hours with proper efforts to pick up freelance work, to apply for jobs I didn't want, at companies I didn't care about, and to generally try and find the means to care for myself if Michael decided to leave me. If he decided to marry Nicolás when I eventually told him I didn't want to be his trophy husband. After four days, which felt so very lonely and bleak that I began to drink my way through them, gently, putting whiskey in my coffees (I'd stopped with the milk phase by this point), Michael came home at a reasonable hour. He had a look on his face that I'd never seen before. Like a naughty child, caught with his hand in the cookie jar.

Michael, look, I said. This wedding.

Oh don't. Please? Let's not right now. He sat down heavily at the kitchen table. I got up and poured us both a wine. It seemed like we both needed one.

What's going on?

I have something I need to tell you. Michael put his hand across his forehead as if he was getting a migraine. I immediately thought – this is it. He's chosen Nicolás, the wedding I didn't even agree to is off. It was all panning out how I'd imagined. I felt relief.

What is it?

I had a call from the hospital today. Hetty has been admitted to intensive care.

I didn't feel my mouth move, but I think I spoke. I could taste pennies in the back of my throat. I wondered what I was supposed to feel, or to ask, in a moment like this. These are the moments they put in films and TV shows. I could infer the correct reaction from that. Stunned silence?

She's contracted an infection. An ambulance was called for her last night, but for some fucking reason I was only called this afternoon.

I knew what the reason was. It was because I'd told the home that in absolutely no circumstances were they to contact either of us, for anything at all to do with Hetty. Unless – and only if – she was dead and needed removing. I'd had them delete my number. That had been a complex conversation to have with the receptionist, but I'd made myself understood eventually. I hadn't realised they'd even got Michael's. It made sense, though. He visited her so often; he'd always taken their strange little alliance very seriously.

I'm going to drive to the hospital now. Are you ready to leave?

Michael pushed his wine away across the table and stood up, scrubbing his hands through his hair. He looked older, suddenly. I could see two new greys in his hairline that he'd not yet plucked. That wasn't like him.

I'm not coming, I said.

Don't be fucking stupid. She's really ill. Put your shoes on.

I'm not coming Michael. I mean it.

He stood there looking at me for a minute. It felt like much longer. I took a sip of my wine and looked back at him.

Fine, he said. You're going to regret this. I know you will.

He left.

That night I ran myself a bath. I drank the rest of the wine. I masturbated in front of the mirror. I ate a whole box of champagne truffles I'd found in the cupboard – a gift from someone at some point. I dangled out of the kitchen window, wearing my towelling robe, and smoked a joint the poet had given me. As I knelt by the open window, vaguely trying to keep the weed smoke out of the house, I kept thinking about the house I grew up in. It had French doors. I could picture them in such detail, imagine the texture of every pane of glass under my fingertips. I could see my breath on the glass, a small cloud, a child's breath. When I'd been 'naughty' as Hetty would put it, although in reality, I'd done fuck all – I was this meek, sad little kid – but when she thought I'd been bad, or when she was drunk – whichever – she'd throw open the French doors and make me kneel on the runners. I'd have to kneel like this for hours, with my arms straight out to the sides. It was hard to balance, and the sharp metal and plastic of the doorframe broke my skin and left purple bruises that I'd watch turn yellow over the following days. Bruises that I'd press with my fingertips to see what I could feel. Sometimes she'd place books on my head, to see how long I could balance them there. To her credit, I have excellent posture to this day. *I am frightened of her downstream.* Repentance, she called it. I've made my peace. I have nothing left to repent for. I've not told Michael about any of this, of course. I don't think about it often, not now. But for some reason that night I couldn't shake the memory.

When I'd eventually sobered up from my drunken bath, when I'd slathered myself in moisturiser and dressed myself in some of Michael's fresh jogging bottoms and an old Pogues t-shirt, I sat down at the desk and got out my laptop. Get your bum on the seat, was what the poet had said. She hadn't said anything about doing it sober. I could smell ylang-ylang and latex. My fingertips were wrinkled up as I pressed them into the keys.

Kingfisher

You see, it's like this —
for instance, a ripple
For instance:
some birds don't land
their whole lives

The way I see it is —
they only break to prove dough
to keeve shell
to be broken by down
Like this: a body, hewn.

23.

Michael didn't come home from the hospital that night. He didn't sleep in the bed next to me, and the shower wasn't steamed up when I stumbled in to pee the next morning. When I looked at my phone, I didn't have any missed calls, or any text messages. I made myself tea and toast. I had an urge to put on some music but felt somehow that it would be too much like I was in a film. This is the bit they always miss out of the films. The quiet bit, the bit where you just exist. I tided up my mess from the night before, I put the dishwasher on. The poet phoned me.

Hello, I said.

Hello, she said back.

How delicious it was to have someone say hello to me for a change.

I think my mother may have died, I said.

Christ, she said. I could hear that she'd stopped walking. I could hear her breathe.

What do you mean 'you think'?

Well, Michael left to see her in intensive care last night. He's not back and I've heard nothing.

That doesn't mean she's dead.

True. But I think she is. I didn't dream anything at all last night.

I didn't find out for definite until that evening. I spent the day in a daze, applying to more jobs that I didn't want. I didn't write, it didn't even occur to me to do so. Michael came home with a crumpled-up face. The sort of face someone does when they don't really know how to do emotions. I imagined him in the 'elevator' on his way up to the flat, practising his sad face in the mirror.

What happened then? I said.

I was drinking again. It had occurred to me that I was an adult and didn't have a stable job, so to be honest drinking was actually a very logical reaction to my circumstances. I was drinking neat rum like a pirate and had drunk enough of it that I felt like I needed an eye patch. I kept closing my left eye as Michael spoke, so that I could focus on his face.

Michael was talking for a very long time, telling me about infection rates and complications and blood clots and at one point something about compensation, which I didn't follow at all. He tried to take my glass of rum away from me, but I held onto it so hard that it spilled across the table. He was crying when he mopped it up and saying things like he couldn't believe what he was saying, things like how terrible a person he was for doing this when this awful thing had just happened. I didn't quite understand what thing it was that he was doing, aside from mopping up spilt rum, which there was certainly no point crying over. I also didn't really understand what terrible thing had happened, because I felt as if I'd been carrying a library's worth of heavy books on my head, trying to make them all balance, and in the space of two days they'd all been lifted away. The weight had been lifted away. Michael said he would stay that night because I was clearly too drunk, then he would pack his things tomorrow, but I didn't really understand what he meant because I was a pirate standing on the deck of my ship and the stormy seas were throwing me about, but it was okay because I would never have to smell that combination of TCP and Angostura bitters again. Michael made me drink herbal tea and get into bed. He put *Friends* on, for some insane reason, and curled up behind me, burying his face into my neck. I still didn't quite know what was going on, but I felt warm and content and fell asleep to the sound of canned laughter. I didn't dream at all that night either.

As I'm sure you will have guessed, the flat was empty when I woke up the next day. Michael's chargers had all disappeared, and the wardrobe door was slightly open. I could see that some of his clothes were missing. I could see myself in that mirror, my hair wild, my face still tanned. I felt almost okay for a moment, but soon my stomach betrayed me. I had to run to the bathroom to be violently sick. My stomach muscles were flexed and taut when I was done. I looked thin, when I looked in the mirror. My hip bones were protruding. So, this was it. I suppose in many ways I'd got exactly what I wanted. I cleaned my teeth and wobbled back to bed. The kitchen stank of rum, I couldn't face going in there and trying to make tea. When I checked my phone, I had two missed calls from the poet. It was late, I'd missed our usual morning call. I couldn't face calling her back, not like this. I phoned Jess. She didn't answer. I text her our code. She phoned me back immediately.

What the hell is going on? I'm in meetings all day.

I told her.

Fucking hell. Right. Let me move some stuff around and I'll be over.

I turned over and tried to sleep. It evaded me, so instead I lay perfectly still, trying to keep my roiling stomach calm. I could still see myself in the mirror. When Jess arrived a couple of hours later, I hadn't moved. She let herself in, she has a key.

Stinks in here, she said, as she sat on the bed next to me.

She was wearing an emerald-green wrap dress with a smart jacket. Her tits were bursting out of the top, as they always do.

What happened then, pumpkin? She smoothed the hair out of my face.

I don't know. Michael left. That's probably good. Hetty died, also probably good.

You shouldn't say that.

You're right, I shouldn't. But it's true.

This whole place stinks of rum and sadness. I'll run you a bath, I can't sit in this.

I heard her put the bath on, and bang about opening all the windows. I still stayed completely still. Perhaps if I stayed like this, if I didn't accept the passing of time, if I just refused to join in with this new reality, then I could stop it. I could still feel Michael's arms around me from last night. He'd been holding me so tightly. The radio was blasting in the kitchen. Jess appeared with water and paracetamol, which she watched me swallow like a stern nurse.

Bath – she said, and clomped back out again in her heeled boots. I obeyed her instruction.

The water was boiling hot. Women always wash in such hot water. Hetty always bathed me in water that left my skin pink and sore. I lay there completely still until Jess banged on the door.

Are you washing? she said.

No, I said.

I'm coming in.

Jess sat on the loo and watched me in the bath. I didn't feel the need to hide my nakedness from her, as I once perhaps would have. It didn't seem to matter. Jess passed me my expensive shampoo, made me wash and condition my hair. She made me use a face scrub with ground up peach pit in it. It didn't smell like peaches. I wanted to smell tangerines and ice cream. When she was convinced that I'd washed myself sufficiently, Jess passed me a fluffy towel. She instructed me to shave, said she would pick out some clothes for me. I didn't know why, or what for, but I did as I was told. It was a relief not to have to decide anything. When I got out of the bath, I saw that she'd laid out my best jeans on the bed, the ones I'd worn to the fish restaurant. I put them on, with a long-sleeved cotton t-shirt. I needed long sleeves to pull down over my hands. When I stepped into the kitchen, I saw that she'd cleaned it, top to bottom. She handed me a coffee with milk and sugar.

You need to eat something, she said.

Probably, I replied. But I don't want to.

Would you just eat a banana? For me?

Okay. I can do that.

I ate the banana slowly; it was cloying and thick in my mouth.

Good boy, well done.

I made a face.

You know I'll always look after you, she said softly.

I did know it, but for some reason it made me angry so I said nothing.

We should go to the hospital, chicken. When you're ready. There will be paperwork to fill out. And perhaps you will want to see her?

I never want to see her.

I didn't speak to the poet at all for three whole days. She rang me in the mornings, as had been our routine, and I slept through the calls, or I didn't answer them. I didn't feel able to step into the space I shared with her. I suppose I was probably meant to be thinking about Hetty, about her alone in that hospital bed, visited only by Michael, a man who repulsed her. To think about what her last moments might have been like, to think about whether she let Michael hold her hand, at the end. But I didn't think about her at all. I thought about my father.

I was twelve when he died. He'd been ill for nearly two years by that point. And he'd left Hetty. The greatest insult, of all his insults to her, as she saw it. He paid for excellent private care, rented a beautiful house to die in. Her final punishment, for both of us, was not to bring me to see him. I didn't get to see him get thin. I didn't get to smell the scent of cigars as he smoked by the window (against doctor's orders, as he would've told me, winking). I didn't get to watch his skin become papery and flake off him like pastry. I didn't get to watch bruises form on his wrists from the lightest of touches. I didn't get to see his eyes get bloodshot from the effort of coughing. I heard it though. Every Sunday, we were permitted one phone call. Ten minutes a week, for nearly two years, until he died. I would hear his breathless voice, hear it change, hear it morph into that of an old man, older than his years. I didn't get to smell Old Spice, to see his shaving kit in the bathroom, to bring him the chocolate he liked. I didn't get to pass him his cigar clipper.

Repentance. I had none left.

For those few days I existed in a liminal space. In one hand I held a handful of my father's trousers as we walked through a market, in the other I gripped the glass I was holding, the bedsheets, a cigarette. When I walked through the flat (kitchen, bathroom, bed) I stayed in step with his loafers. His eyes were brown like the hawk and brown like mine and I held onto him tightly. I thought about what he might think of me now, what he'd say about the poet and about love and what he could teach me about what grows and what dies.

I took random pills from the medicine cabinet and I drank whatever spirits were lying around and I trailed about in an undone dressing gown with all the windows of the flat open to let in the sound. I saw him at every stage of his life all in one, the image flickering before me had his grey hairs and the blonde of him as a child, the strands changing as I looked to the brown I saw in the mirror. I took long baths and watched my fingertips wrinkle. I lay on the floor of the living room and waited until my skin dried.

I'd like to say that I planned Hetty's funeral, but that would be a lie. In fact, in a gesture of complete and pure generosity, Jess planned it. She picked the funeral directors, made the guestlist (which was miniscule), took the lengthy calls with the crematorium, rented me a suit (I don't own one), found us a relatively non-offensive wine bar nearby to drink in afterward. She did this gracefully and almost invisibly. In doing so, she taught me a little about what love is supposed to look like. Plus, she's excellent at admin. Jess had it all nailed down within 48 hours. It was very impressive. I made one decision. I chose the flowers. Rosa Sun Flare.

You'll have to invite the poet, she told me. It's Friday, 11am. I've told everyone else.

I sent the poet a text. *I think I need you*, it said. *Will you be there? Of course*, she replied. *Will bring whiskey. Kiss kiss.*

*My lips will remain swollen
with the ways I could love.*

Jordan Hayward

24.

Ishia brought us tea. It absolutely, definitely wasn't her job to do so, but in an expression of solace and awkwardness, she disappeared into the kitchen and came back holding a tray with two steaming, floral mugs. When someone dies that's the only safe action, of course. I've never felt more British in my life. There was a saucer of hobnobs and chocolate digestives on the tray, presumably from Ishia's own biscuit tin.

I'll leave you to it, she said. Come find me if you need anything.

No tea for her. She had other, important things to do, no doubt. Other, living residents to care for. Residents who, I hoped, wouldn't subject her to the blithe intolerance my mother had favoured. Had favoured. Past tense. I was having some trouble with tenses. I kept mixing them up, placing Hetty in the past and the present and also sometimes in the future, where she had no business being.

I looked about the room. I'd spent very little time here, during the three years it had been my mother's home. Our visits were spent downstairs, where it was easier for Hetty to pretend to be lady of the manor, rather than a vulnerable citizen lucky enough to have a bit of cash. My father's ashes were on the mantlepiece. *My father's hand was in mine and I could hear the tinny radio playing Christmas music.* He would be coming home with me. He could watch my mistakes now, instead of hers. Jessica was already in the wardrobe, digging through Hetty's terrible suits. The air was thick with death, although she'd not died in this room. I opened the window.

You can sell this, she said. The older stuff is mostly designer. Stick it on eBay.

I'd rather stick it on a fire, I said.

I munched a hobnob and immediately regretted it, as the oats became gluey in my mouth. I didn't think I'd be able to swallow it.

I suppose I'll add that to my list of jobs then. Jess rolled her eyes and made a note on her pad.

No, sorry Jess, you've done too much already. I'm a dick. I'll get to this stuff eventually.

I'll make you a deal – I'll sell the clothes and take a cut. 20% sound okay?

Ouch. You're never off duty are you.

Fuck no.

It's all yours. Take all the profit. Payment for services rendered.

I went to the window. It was high, probably too high for Hetty to be able to see out of it from her wheelchair. I wondered if the view was good enough for her to stop pretending to be a cripple and get up and have a look. I imagined her there, leaning her hands on the windowsill for balance.

The gardens were beautiful. Wild and beautiful, thick swathes of lush greenery in the beds, most of the flowers gone over now. The lawn was neat and mowed with symmetrical stripes. Someone took pride in that lawn. I couldn't remember the last time I took pride in something. I knew I was supposed to be filling boxes, allocating things to different piles: keep, sell, bin, charity shop, but I couldn't quite bring myself to touch anything. The room was immaculate. Neat, clean, everything away in drawers and cupboards with shining brass handles and wood that smelled of beeswax. There was a notepad on a side table with what looked like potential crossword answers in her tiny handwriting. The bunch of roses I'd bought for her when she was in hospital, cradled by baby's breath, were hanging upside down in one window. She couldn't have reached to hang them like that. Which meant she must have asked someone to preserve them for her. That felt uncomfortable. I'd meant them as some kind of childish insult, in a way, a message telling her I was still on dad's side, that I always would be. But she'd kept them. They'd meant something to her. I'm sure she knew they weren't an expression of love. But that was very like her. Hetty always liked the sharp things in life. Perhaps now I should keep them? That wasn't much to take with me, really, was it? My father's ashes and some dead roses.

Right, said Jess, and began unrolling some binbags. She whipped one open with a loud crack. A sonic boom. Let's get on with it, shall we?

Having a friend as efficient as Jessica meant that the death admin took an extraordinarily short amount of time. She even delegated, having her PA fill in the paperwork for the probate applications, including for the death certificate. I just had to turn up and sign it all, like some kind of ghoulish businessman.

We spent that whole afternoon in Hetty's room. Jess had everything separated into piles. She arranged for the furniture I didn't want to be collected by a local charity. She asked Ishia if she was willing to dispose of the rubbish, and she obliged. She kept some of Hetty's jewellery herself. I was glad there was something she wanted. I planned on selling most of it, except the engagement ring, which had belonged to my father's family. I knew he'd wanted it back for years, so I felt some small satisfaction in keeping it, finally. I found a silver chain, in with all her pearls and things, and strung the ring onto it. Jess fastened it around my neck. I felt a touch odd, with diamonds and a sapphire flashing about my throat, but I also felt that it suited me. Sapphires are a variety of corundum, a crystalised form of aluminium oxide. The word also refers to a small hummingbird with shining blue or violet colours in its plumage. Every time I touched it dad's eyes flickered before me. His thin skin, his heavy veins. His smell.

I kept going outside for cigarettes and trailing the edge of the perfect lawn. Jessica did most of the work. I am never the one to do most of the work, and for once I felt guilty about that. I could smell the grass; smell the sweat of the gardener I imagined tending the perfect lawn. When we had finished for the day, Jess took me out for sushi. There was a lump in my throat that was getting bigger by the minute. I couldn't swallow my tuna sashimi, had to wash everything down with too much beer. Tomorrow was Friday. The funeral was at 11am. I knew it was wrong, but I couldn't wait. I couldn't wait to cremate my mother so that I could stand next to the poet and hold her hand.

25.

September began on the day I cremated my mother. It was autumn. A new season in more ways than one. Jessica stayed over at the flat the night before. I'd heard nothing from Michael since he left that night while I was asleep. I woke up to my phone flashing, the poet's name on the screen.

Hello, she said. I could listen to her say hello for a million years. Hello, hello. Hello my love.

I'm sorry, I said, in response. I didn't mean to ignore you. I've not really been with it.

Don't be sorry, please. When my mother died, I went up a mountain and ignored everyone for a week. It was all very dramatic.

It feels like a drama, doesn't it? I feel like I'm in a drama, like I'm in a story.

Perhaps you are. Would you still like me to come today?

I want nothing more in the world.

The weather was gorgeous on the day I cremated my mother. *Sumptuous.* Sunlight stabbed through the trees into the misty air, creating a stage of spotlights for the funeral party to glide through. And glide we did, but I've not got to that part yet. The first part is when I got dressed. Jess made me drink coffee and eat half a croissant with her. My hair had finally grown long enough to put up, and I tied it at the back of my head. A few strands fell down by my face. Hetty would have hated it. Jessica had hired me a beautiful and understated black suit. I wore my best white shirt, glossy black Chelsea boots. No tie. Hetty would have been horrified. Jess fastened the chain with the engagement ring around my neck.

The sapphire glinted against my tanned chest. Blue feathers. I kept touching it with shaking fingers, terrified it would disappear. I rubbed black kohl under my eyes. I smoked a cigarette by the kitchen window and wore all my silver rings. I took some of the dried gypsophila from the flowers I'd bought for Hetty and tucked it into my lapel. The buzzer rang: our taxi was here.

I sunburned my nose on the day I cremated my mother. I didn't have any sun cream, blue or otherwise, and no matter where I stood, the sun found me. The sun was always searching for me.

The poet was waiting outside the crematorium. She was holding a bunch of yellow lilies, and I couldn't figure out how she'd known that the theme of the day was yellow. Nobody else had arrived yet. There wouldn't be many guests. Hetty had alienated her own family, and what was left of my father's family were far too busy growing old in Italy to attend the funeral of a woman that they, at best, felt indifferent about. I was expecting to see someone from the residential home, most likely Ishia. A couple of ex-colleagues of Hetty's, from the days when she worked in the admin office for the symphony orchestra. Jessica embraced the poet as if they'd known each other for years. They led me inside and sat me down at the front. The crematorium had wooden benches that looked like pews, even though it wasn't a church. The edges of the wood had a layer of dust in the cracks. They looked ignored. The room smelled of Febreze. Jessica went off to host, professional until the end, and the poet stayed with me. She held my hand tightly, as I'd hoped that she would.

Just as things were about to begin, Michael walked into the room. He was holding hands with a beautiful young man that could only be Nicolás. He smiled at me weakly, and they both sat down at the back. They were both wearing blue suits, which annoyed me, because aside from them everyone had stuck to the chosen aesthetic: black, white, yellow. In a moment of weakness,

I'd conceded to Jess that we should play Albinoni's Adagio in G minor as the curtains closed on the coffin. I regretted that later when I found myself weeping kohl lines down my face and the poet had to pass me a tissue.

I didn't have time to think about any of it, however, because then the celebrant began talking and all I could hear was a buzzing sound and all I could see was the gleam of the mahogany coffin that contained my mother.

26.

On the first day of autumn, on the day I cremated my mother, when I was done weeping at the singing crescendo of strings, when I'd wiped my nose and the poet had cleaned the kohl from my cheeks, Jessica and the poet led me out into the September sunshine. They flanked me like bodyguards, and although I could see Michael and Nicolás out of the corner of my eye, I did not focus on them. I stepped onto the cobbles of the forecourt and looked down at the shine on my boots. I rolled a cigarette and smoked it quickly. I couldn't think of anything else to do with my hands. The poet stayed silent, gripping my arm with one hand. Jessica smiled at me encouragingly. People had begun to exit behind me.

I'm going to rally the troops, said Jess. Give directions to the pub and what not. Okay?

Okay. The poet answered for me. We're going to take a little walk in the gardens.

Good idea.

I was being shepherded. Coaxed. Directed. I followed their lead.

The poet walked me onto a small path that wove between uncomfortably neat flowerbeds. All the plants looked awkward, breathless, as if they were wearing corsets. I glanced behind me and saw that Jessica was talking to Michael and Nicolás. They were both watching me walk away and doing that thing people do with their faces when someone has died. A sort of grimace at the fact that they were now all roped into this little play. That they all had to join in with this amateur production of human emotion. Everyone looked rather dashing. There might not be many guests, but those that were there were all either beautiful or richly dressed or both.

Hetty would've liked that. Everyone was gliding into the sunlight and the poet led me down the path until we found a bench, out of the eyeline of the doors to the crematorium.

Let's sit, she said. I obeyed.

She pulled a small bottle of Irish whiskey from her bag and handed it to me. I took a long pull and handed it back. She drank some too. I rolled us both a cigarette. The poet didn't say anything, and I thought about how much better she was at emotions than I was, than most people I knew were. Here was a moment where whiskey and silence were exactly what was required. She settled into it like a bird fluffing her feathers. She leaned back against the bench and put her head back. There was a gentle breeze and her hair fluttered and she closed her eyes.

It's Monday, isn't it? I asked, already knowing the answer.

It is, she said.

Can I be there?

I'm praying you will be.

Of course. I wouldn't be anywhere else.

I'd like you to bring ice cream. And some cherries. And a crossword book.

And whiskey?

She laughed. I'm not sure what the hospital would think of that.

She took another swig and handed the bottle to me.

It's going to be okay, you know. It's going to be okay for both of us.

The pub had no soft furnishings, and those awful high-back pleather chairs you see sometimes. The kind of chairs that scream of giving up, scream of someone not just with bad taste, but with no capability of forming an aesthetic of any kind. It was loud and clattering, and in an adjacent room was some kind of party. There were children, with tense women in fake tan and summer dresses from Forever 21 trying to control them. As we passed the door of the function room, I leaned in and pulled it closed. I didn't have the mental space to consider whether it was rude to do so, but more importantly the sound of happy children and sad women would make me cry. I had only just regained control of my face and seemingly was about to share a drink with Michael and Nicolás, so I needed all my faculties.

Jessica led us to a large table under a once-pretty bay window, now painted shut with messy layers of eggshell. There was a reserved sign on it and a small wooden tub containing ketchup and mayonnaise sachets. The poet signalled me to sit and shuffled in after me. Jessica was still conducting the ceremony and waving to people. Ishia came and joined us, already nursing half a Yorkshire blonde. I looked at the golden liquid, imagining sand running through it, a timer filled with inoffensive and gentle beer to carry her through the absolute minimum socially acceptable time she had to sit with us. An hourglass of ale. She smiled at me with her eyes and her mouth.

Your mother will be missed, she said.

No, she won't, I said. The poet looked at me angrily.

She will, actually, Ishia said mildly. Although probably not the way you'd expect. We've a couple of really difficult residents. Hetty kept them in line for us. They were all scared of her. I've not been told to go back to where I came from once since she's been there. One chap used to spit at me, but he had a crush on your mother, so he's been on best behaviour.

Right, I said. Wow. Well, you've told me then, haven't you?

Jess appeared with whiskey for me and the poet.

Ishia raised her glass. To Hetty, she said. The queen of the intolerant.

I tried to drink but it made me laugh so hard that whiskey came out of my nose, and I started coughing. Naturally, at that moment Michael and Nicolás arrived. It sounded like the party next door were singing 'Happy Birthday'. Why don't we do cakes at funerals? You could blow out one candle for every year the person was alive. The final count. I could hear screeching and singing and shouting and I could smell old chip fat.

This is nice! said Michael as he sat down.

He was being forcibly jovial, like an alcoholic dressed as Santa Claus.

We are all together. I'm sure that's what she would have wanted.

I could feel a giggle rising in my chest again, so I put my face in my drink. Hetty would not have wanted this. The idea of raising a glass to her in a mediocre pub felt like the final insult. Most especially when Michael and I were here with our second partners – our mistresses? misters? – or whatever they were. I wished I'd had the chance to tell her all this. I wished she could be there to see it. I could tell that I was smiling like an idiot, but I couldn't make my face do anything normal for a funeral. I wasn't wake-appropriate.

I looked at Nicolás, because not looking at him was like trying not to look at a sunset and because I was sure that he was feeling far worse about being there than I was about his presence. I found him looking right back at me. He has incredibly long eyelashes. Brown eyes, almost black. Michael certainly has a type.

I am so sorry, he said. He spread both hands out in front of him, fingers apart.

I am sorry for all. For all of it.

I realised, to my annoyance, that I liked him.

That's okay, I said. I mirrored his hands, spreading my fingers in front of me. I'm sorry too.

Jessica arrived at the table, shepherding my mother's old colleagues and a couple of strays.

Here – she said, handing them over.

Everyone shuffled round the booth to make room.

We were supposed to have that room in there (Jess pointed viciously at the function room) but they double booked and didn't tell me. I've had them bring us some tapas bits as an apology, and the next round is on them, so if you could all order something expensive, I'd appreciate it. Okay?

We all nodded. She clomped back off to the bar to continue negotiating with the harangued manager, who could only be about twenty-one years old. I felt I should probably rescue him, but I was now hemmed in by the poet, by Ishia and Michael and Nicolás, and by two old women whose names I did not know. I set about drinking my whiskey. Tentative conversation sprang up around the table. The poet tried to engage the older women while Ishia spoke to Michael. Nicolás looked about him with a fearful expression that I imagined on my own face. Honestly, it wasn't that bad. Soon a waitress brought over some hummus, carrot sticks and lukewarm pittas. I watched Jess waving her arms about at the manager for a bit like it was a silent disco. Some chips arrived, some mozzarella sticks and jalapeno poppers. Nicolás picked one up with curiosity.

I wouldn't, I said.

Gracias, he said, and smiled in a way that made his eyes crinkle.

The poet took my hand under the table.

I spent Saturday stoned, under a blanket on the sofa. Jessica left around dinnertime the night before, having checked I was settled. Her shift was officially over. I played about on my phone, fiddled with the apps for a bit before deciding that would be too depressing – even in my current state. The poet phoned me. She'd left after about an hour at the pub. Fair enough. I put her on speakerphone and leant my head back.

Hello, she said. How are you faring?

Middling to good.

So, she said. Tomorrow.

Tomorrow.

I want to sleep outside. For my last night. I'd like you to join me.

Of course.

Come to the house. You can help me pack up the tent and make some food.

I fell asleep after the call, waking on the sofa to an overly loud TV at 3am. I shuffled off to bed but lay there awake all night thinking about Hetty and Ishia and Michael and Nicolás and about writing, writing writing writing.

27.

When I drove to the poet's house that Sunday, I doubled back on myself. I drove halfway back home before turning the car again, returning to my original journey. I was slow and got beeped at more than once. I couldn't tell you what I was afraid of, and if I'm honest I'm not sure I was feeling anything at all. I drank a mango smoothie from the M&S in the petrol station. I was an orphan now, technically. It wasn't the same as being orphaned as a child, of course, and I wondered whether anything about it had fundamentally changed me. I didn't think it had. I was frightened of arriving at the poet's house in this new, numb state, and of not being able to feel anything when I was with her. Today was her last full day of being alive, as she saw it, and I felt it my duty to make the most of it. I turned the car around and nearly went home because I didn't think I had it in me to make anyone feel good, least of all myself. However, when I'd parked up at the house and she opened the door to me, I discovered I was wrong.

The joy I felt leaping in my chest as I walked towards her must have been writ on my face, because she beamed back at me. I embraced her at the door and lifted her tiny form, carrying her to the sofa where we first made love. I began pulling her clothes from her awkwardly, as she mumbled protests about the curtains being open through our kisses. At that moment I knew that I needed to be as close to her as I could get, I knew that if I wasn't inside her as soon as possible I would suddenly see all the realities of our lives that I'd been so desperately running from since I'd met her.

I love you, I told her.

I know you do, she replied.

And did you feel it, in your heart, how it pertained to everything?
And have you too finally figured out what beauty is for?
And have you changed your life?

Mary Oliver

28.

~ Two months later ~

The first frost. There's always that one morning when the cold renders the world quiet. The birds take stock. The tarmac glints like cracked geode, crystals spilling over to form on the blades of grass. I'd bought myself a cheap car, a battered Vauxhall, being as I no longer had access to Michael's. He'd been gone for weeks now, but we'd still not really discussed what we would do about the flat. We still paid half each. It was as if he was paying a fee in order not to speak to me. I'd left him a couple of messages but heard nothing back. My fingers ached as I scraped the ice from the windscreen. It collected on my gloves. I scraped some into little piles, lines. I'd not taken any drugs since that night at the fish restaurant. Well, not the illegal kind anyway. I was still drinking though. It seemed fine. Everyone drinks in winter, don't they? It's warming.

My journey from the flat to the hospital felt normal now. A commute. A commute I'd undertaken alongside my real commute, for I had a job, too. A job and a car. How much had changed in the passage between autumn and winter. I was back at the university. Not a teaching position, but admin in the English department. Three days per week. The poet's colleagues all took it as a given that I was with her. In what context they thought this was I do not know, but they passed on messages through me, warm wishes, occasional cakes, or cards. Weed brownies, once, which had done wonders for her tiny and waning appetite. She was beginning her second cycle. The first had been four weeks, and then a break. This would be a brutal six. I spoke about it like a veteran, using the shorthand. The nurses knew me by name and flirted with me in a maternal way. I flexed my fingers on the steering wheel. My gloves were black leather. I took a packet of Marlboro Lights from the glovebox and lit one. I cracked the window, felt the cold hit my cheek, felt the moisture gather as I exhaled smoke and vapour.

I parked, I signed in, I walked to where I knew she would be. The high-backed blue chairs. The cheery posters on the walls. The TV in the corner playing reruns of Come Dine with Me. The boxes of crayons and scrap paper for the people with children. The piles of old newspapers and magazines from the early 2010s. The scuffed floor, the wide, plastic windows. And there she was. My kingfisher. Small and frail and gloriously feathered, despite now lacking any hair on her head. Having seen too many films, I'd wanted to shave my head in solidarity when she began to lose hers again (we always had to say again, she would let nobody forget that she'd done this before). The poet forbade me, and instead I had to promise not to cut it at all. It was getting really long. I had begun to wear it in a French braid, after she taught me how. Three sections, woven in and out, adding more each time. Three sections like the three sections of my life: home, work, her.

I've got one really good one, and one shit one. Can you cope? I said to her, as I dragged over a spare chair and sat down.

The poet gulped and leaned back. She was feeling sick. That meant they'd not long started.

Yes, she said. But I want two good ones next time.

Okay, I said, and pulled out my laptop and a thin green carrier bag. Inside it was a strawberry Calipo. Slightly melted, just the right amount. I peeled off the lid and handed it to her. She stuck her tongue in the top, then held it against her forehead.

Right, you ready?

She nodded.

Question one: in terms of volume, what is the largest freshwater lake in the USA?

Hi Dad, I said as I walked into the flat.

He didn't answer me, obviously, because he is ashes. But he's here now, sat on the kitchen counter, next to the kettle. I talk to Hetty too, who is now also ashes, but I keep her in the bedroom. I want her to watch me when I take men home. I do that quite a lot now. I can't fuck the poet anymore, she's too fragile. I'd like to again, one day. I still think she's magnificent.

Tough one today, I told him. She only got 24/30, which is unheard of for her. For me that would be a good score.

I flipped the kettle on and made myself a shit coffee. I put a little whiskey in it. Irish, of course. The poet kept me in good supply. I poured myself a bowl of cereal.

Aside from the men I brought home, my life had become rather quiet. I spent my evenings reading and actually writing, for a change. The cold had brought with it a stillness, and this stillness allowed me to sit at my desk, with my terrible coffees and my too much alcohol. A collection had begun to tease itself together. Or the beginning drafts had, anyway. I no longer wanted to write about sweat and semen, I was preoccupied with odours of a more feminine kind. And birds, of course. The poet had gifted me birds as if they were an infectious disease. They were in my bloodstream.

In the mornings I took myself off to the gym, before taking that familiar route to the university. Unless I was at the hospital, of course. Or at the poet's flat, where I spent much of my time. She was based there full-time now, as much as she loved her big white house and its walks. But the flat was smaller, easier to navigate. I'd moved her spare bed down into the living room, next to the fire. She didn't like having it there, because it made her feel like a sick person, but then she was a sick person, so there was little she could do about that. I'd carried it down one afternoon while she sat in the kitchen with her friend Laurel. I could hear them whispering together as I lugged various bits of wood down the stairs. I couldn't hear what they said. After my evenings there I would cycle home, rather than drive. I was quite healthy, for the most part, aside from the smoking and the booze.

I flicked my plait over my shoulder. I kept my beard slightly longer than I once had, to try and balance it out.

You should see me now Dad. I look like a right girl.

Dad and I are walking through a market and he's holding up different fruits for me. He shows me exactly how soft a mango should feel, but I shake my head. He juggles with oranges and I laugh. I am taller than him and up to his ribcage all at once. I take a grape from a bunch and eat it
   and the stall owner shouts at us and we run away.
   He is sat on his shelf and I can see his hawk eyes.

That evening I had nothing on my plate but an opportunity to write. It's funny how such an opportunity can be stifling. I did all the right things, I made myself another pot of proper coffee (and didn't make it Irish), I put on some classical piano (solos, gentle, tinkling), I cleared my desk of clutter. I sat down on my new ergonomic chair. The coffee was sweet, and strong enough to stain the cup. I tapped my fingers on the desk. It had once lived in our kitchen, and it was where my father would sit in the mornings, drinking coffee as I was doing now. Eating an orange, removing the peel in one long coil. The patina was golden with age, and it always felt warm to the touch. Aside from drinking, I only knew one way to calm the roiling in my head. I put my pen to the page and scribbled a few notes, enough that I could pretend I'd done some work. Then I stood, put on my jacket, and walked out of the door.

The bar was small and dark. The walls were mostly painted charcoal grey, and the furniture was heavy, lots of metal and dark wood. I placed my elbows on the bar and looked around. It wasn't busy, on a weeknight, but there were enough people here that I knew I'd find someone. I'd been doing this a lot recently. I wanted the poet,

I wanted to be in her arms, and I wanted her to love me, something she still had not said. I'd never been in this position before, or at least, not quite like this. I'd always been the one who was in most demand. If not emotionally then at least physically. And I was always the one to leave, too, until Michael at least. My fingers on the bar were trembling. It was as if the weight of the grey walls was pressing down upon me, so that every tiny muscle I possessed was shaking with the strain. I was a leaf in a storm. I was trying to hold on, but I didn't know what to.

There. Across the way. He would do. He looked like he had strong arms. I approached him and sat down. Made my sparkling conversation. While I spoke to him, I could feel the rocks in my belly compressing. Shrinking from the pressure of the grey walls. Soon they would be pounded into dust. I followed the man into the toilet and snorted whatever it was he held out to me on the corner of his credit card. It turned out to be ketamine, which wasn't what I was expecting. The grey walls turned from rock to water as I returned to my seat at the bar. I placed my feet carefully, aware that the floor could liquify at any moment.

He bought me drinks. My conversation was less than sparkling. My hands stopped shaking. We stayed until the bar closed. When I next got back up off that chair my legs had dissolved. The undertow was pulling at my trousers like tiny hands.

We stepped outside into the shrill air. I regretted not wearing a scarf. My neck felt tender and open; I could not stop thinking about all the arteries and veins in there. Who designed necks? They are so vulnerable. I put two fingers up and took my pulse. I stumbled into an alley to take a piss. When my fly was down, I could almost feel him come up behind me, but I ignored it. It wasn't a night to be listening to instincts. The next thing I felt was my face against wet brick as he slammed me into the wall.

What do you want, he breathed into my ear.

To disappear, I said, as his heavy stone hands tore at my underwear.

He was stone, I was stone, I was water, I was a river.

When I returned home in the early hours, I took a shower, rubbed some Sudocrem into the graze across my cheek. I felt clean and fresh like a little baby, like the rawness I felt was from a newness. I made another pot of coffee. It was sweet, and strong enough to stain the cup. I wrote for as long as I could keep myself conscious, then collapsed into bed.

29.

I am only a young man now if I die suddenly. You have to be the man of the house, they said. The world is at your feet, they said. I stamped all over it. A pile of bricks is not the same as a house. If nobody does anything with it then it's just a wasteland. *Dad is juggling again and I can't see Hetty at all.* I am not quite a wasteland, but I do have a habit of building walls only to knock them down again.

I was expelled from my sixth form for breaking in after my exams and throwing red paint all over the art block. I think at the time I'd thought the art teacher would appreciate it – my final installation. I'd also been taking a lot of speed and hadn't slept for so long that the hallucinations were creeping in.

That was one wall I tried to batter down, the wall of my intelligence, this abstract thing people kept using as a reason why I should be better than I was, than I am. My plan didn't work, as my English teacher stepped in and had the situation reversed, so that I could take up my university place. He knew what my mother had done to me, so it was partly out of sympathy, but it was also because I'd been sucking him off in the car park and he didn't want to get fired.

Keep the angry boy on side. You don't know what he might do. There have been too many people in my life who wanted to help me.

30.

Jessica, Jessica. I do not deserve my Jessica. That weekend she took me for a Sunday roast. We'd begun spending time together more regularly since the funeral, our relationship developing into something other than alcohol and mean talk. She had shown me what it meant to love, and next to the sweet, tender desert I shared with the poet, Jessica existed concurrently, a slowly beating warmth, a disembodied heart pulsing in the sunshine.

Jessica had begun seeing a new man. I was not impressed. He was her superior at work and had a cruel mouth. Jessica had a history of picking terrible men. Don't we all. It's almost as if most men are terrible.

He's got a big cock though.

Jesus. That's hardly the most important thing, is it?

I took a mouthful of my mushroom wellington, shaking my head, as if I would not have said the same thing not so long ago. But I was a martyr now. An angel.

It's better than nothing.

You deserve better than nothing, I said.

Jess looked livid. I was not supposed to be genuine with her. I was ruining the pact.

He watches TV with me, she said quietly.

That's it?

No, that's not it. He makes me tea how I like it. He texts me in the morning. He doesn't require me to care for him.

The bar is in hell.

You'd know.

So, when will you see him again?

Oh, I don't know. Whenever his wife's next away. Joking, before you start. Anyway, enough about my dusty vagina escapades. Anything from Michael?

Nothing. It hardly matters. As long as I have the flat anyway.

What about *that woman?*

For some reason Jessica had taken to calling the poet this. It sounded mean, but I knew that Jessica liked her. I think she struggled to understand the nature of our relationship. So did I. I questioned whether there was a twist of green in there too. Part of me occasionally wondered whether Jess assumed we'd end up together one day, but I always dismissed it. Part of me wished she was right.

She's started the next round. It's clobbering her already and she's barely begun. Her skin looks a little blue. I can see her veins.

She's Irish, you can see her veins anyway.

Says you.

I bloody do. Besides, I pay good money not to be translucent. She ran her finger down a tastefully tanned arm. Hiding my Celtic roots. Anyway, what about you? Anyone interesting on the horizon?

I thought about that man the other night. Whatever that was, I didn't think it counted.

No, I said. I only have eyes for two women.

Two?

Well, you and her of course. I'm too busy for anything else.

I didn't tell her that I'd spent that whole morning watching adverts for crack sealant and grout cleaner. I needed to be wiped clean, patched together. I didn't have the time to do anything except nothing. I could smell the lies as they came out of my mouth. They smelled like solvents, like bitter medicine for naughty children.

Our usual pilgrimage. My life had so many routines now, I wouldn't have believed it a year ago. After our lazy lunch Jessica walked us to her 4x4. Metallic blue, too big for the road. We climbed in and I switched on the heated seats. It made me feel like I'd wet myself.

The gardens were a short drive away from our chosen pub. The particular bench, the one I'd made a donation for, the one I'd had inscribed with my father's dates, was around a fifteen-minute walk into the grounds. Hetty was a spectre, an invisible energy I couldn't shake. *Dad flew over us, scaring the smaller birds in shrieking bursts from the trees.* We parked up and I pulled on my gloves. I felt sick and heavy with food, my stomach swollen. Jessica took my arm and we wandered down the pathways as she told me more about this awful man, and the excuses she was willing to make for him. The sun beat down enough that I felt sure it would burn my cheeks, the bridge of my nose. It was still cold, the patches of grass that remained in the shade maintained a coating of frost. We found the bench. Jessica smiled and ran a manicured fingernail over the brass plaque.

I would have liked to meet him.

He would've tried to shag you.

Maybe I'd have let him. He wasn't short of a penny.

I sat down and pulled a joint from my jacket pocket. For a while we sat and smoked in silence, hardly having to raise our eyes to take the joint from each other. The green had leached from the grass somewhat, winter had already begun sucking and pulling the life from things. I could see browns, faded mosses. I could hear wings moving, water cracking as it turned into ice. *I was running through the market with my father and we were laughing.*

Look, said Jess, over there –

There were two small deer, stepping slowly through the scrubland. We watched them in silence.

Are you going to bring her here?

No. This was his place. She's already where she belongs.

And where is that?

On top of my wardrobe, next to the spare suitcase.

Was he a bitter man?

My dad? No. Overly generous. The opposite.

Wouldn't you rather end up like him?

I couldn't stop making bread. I'd begun as the weather had started to turn, the golden leaves sparking thoughts of the most perfect golden loaf, and now I couldn't stop. I've never had trouble becoming addicted to something. This was probably one of my healthier somethings.

I didn't eat the bread myself, partly because eating can just as easily become an addiction, and partly because if I were to eat all that bread I'd lose that sharpness of thought, the external validation that comes with a little purposeful starvation. It's all about control. Drinking is about controlling what you feel and smoking is about controlling your hands and if you control what you eat you can, to some extent, control what others think of you.

The other way I did this was to bring the loaves into work and hand them to my colleagues. I'd begun affecting a little extra camp while I was there. It was helped by the long hair, but also, I think I was doing it to protect the poet, somehow. If I was camp, then that meant there could be no nefarious assumptions about the nature of our relationship. I was just a fag, and people could neatly file away our relationship into a box they understood, and therefore not ask me questions I couldn't answer. And if that were the case, I could be more relaxed and honest when I chatted to my new boss, the head of admin for the English department, over lunch, which we ate in a grim little staffroom with dead flies on the windowsill. As we did so, I inevitably thought about my springtime lunches on the metal bench with the poet, about Marks and Spencer smoothies and about iced coffee and stolen kisses, as I watched the rain run down the windows, as I shrugged on my sodden jacket to go out for a cigarette.

Are you married, Saoirse? I asked, as she followed me out under the shelter of my umbrella, that same blue umbrella I'd sheltered the poet under outside the Italian restaurant, all those months ago.

Nope. She pulled a straight from a packet of Lambert and Butler and swiftly lit it, taking the umbrella from my hands so that I could roll.

I do have a man that lives in my house, though, but I'm thinking of getting rid.

Oh yeah, how come?

My fingers were shaking and the rizla was damp. It was taking me too many goes to roll. She looked at it and then back up to me. I pulled out a fresh paper awkwardly and tried again.

He takes more than he gives, she said simply.

I looked at her for more, but she just shrugged, and raised her eyebrows. That was all I was gonna get.

I'm trying to figure out where to scatter my mother's ashes.

I'm sorry, said Saoirse. She sounded like she actually meant it.

Don't worry, I replied. It's not actually sad. She was a terrible person.

Where did she like to be the most? Perhaps that's the best place, somewhere you know she loved.

That's the problem. She didn't like anywhere or anything or anyone. Or, at least, if she did, she never told me.

Well.

Saoirse took a long drag of her cigarette and exhaled through her nose.

I took the umbrella back from her and lit my own. We stood in silence for a few moments, but I could tell she was really thinking about it.

Where was she born?

Oxford. Not very exciting.

I think you find a piece of coastline that you like. If she didn't like anything then it doesn't matter where, really. Then, you can scatter them in the sea. Let the water figure out where to take her so you don't have to. That way, if you ever want to go see her again you can go somewhere you actually like.

I took one of my loaves of bread to the poet's flat. It wasn't for her, as she struggled eating at the moment and could only stomach very specific things: certain ice lollies, gazpacho ordered from a particular restaurant in the city if she was having a good day, small mouthfuls of Weetabix soaked in milk until soggy. The bread was to placate her friend Laurel, for my existence really, which seemed to disgust her.

I kept thinking about what Saoirse said. He takes more than he gives. The poet takes more from me than she gives, but then she has nothing to give, she is ailing, she's fragmented. Hetty only took, and never gave. My father gave and then disappeared, until he didn't and now I see him everywhere. I think Laurel dislikes me because she thinks I'm there to take from the poet, lurking in the shadows waiting for death like some Anna Nicole Smith character. Very silly. Also, and I've not told Laurel this, or the poet for that matter because it's none of their business, but I already have money. What remained of my father's estate, after Hetty did her level best to wipe it out, was left to me. I'd been expecting it to go to somewhere ridiculous, a charity for something inane, or perhaps to the home she'd lived out her final days in, or even to Ishia, the woman who worked there who'd liked her, in some strange way. But no, it went to me, and now sat in my bank account like a big shiny egg just waiting for me to smash it to bits.

If the poet was to die and if she did leave anything to me, I cannot imagine how it would taste. I don't want her big white house if she is not flitting about in it, and I don't want her city crash pad if she is not settled on her perch by the fire. If she was to leave anything to me then I would destroy it all. But she won't, because she takes more than she gives. And that's what I'm here for, after all. I'm a sub. A masochist.

31.

It's a beautiful loaf.

The poet was sitting on one end of the sofa, with her feet curled up next to her. 6 Music was playing quietly in the background and there was a mug of fruit tea next to her. Today was a good day. The first in a while.

Says you, I said, smiling at her from the floor.

I was starting off a puzzle for her. She doesn't like doing the edges, says they give her vertigo, so I was piecing together the sides of Van Gogh's *Sunflowers*. Then she could take the pieces of orange and yellow in her thin fingers and match them up, remarry stem to stem and leaf to leaf. Petal to petal.

Look, if I could eat then I'd have some, you know that.

Fair enough. I can't argue with someone with cancer. It's not a fair fight.

You've gotta give me that at least.

Always.

So how is the writing going?

It's going. Slowly. Painfully. Death by a thousand cuts. You know, the usual.

She rolled her eyes at me. But not in an unkind way. It still irritated me, though, the fact that because of who she was I always had to take her opinions on my work. And now it was much harder to argue with her, of course. Instead of snapping at her, I got up from the floor and went out to the kitchen. The branches were bare in her back garden. I stood at the sink for a while, staring at them, forgetting why I'd gone in there. There were no birds. I ran the hot tap until it steamed, took a plastic washing up bowl from under the sink and filled it with hot water. Not hot enough to burn, but hot enough to shock. I went to the bathroom and found a soft towel, warm from the radiator, and jasmine-scented shower gel.

I lit the gas fire and placed the bowl of water at the poet's feet. In India, it's a sign of respect to touch someone's feet. They are the lowest part of a person. I am the lowest part of the poet. I unfolded her feet from next to her on the sofa and gently placed them in the water. She stared at me, impassive, except for a little gasp as her skin touched the heat of the water. I took off my silver rings and stacked them carefully on the side table. I seemed to be doing everything very deliberately, moving slowly. I washed her feet, soaping between her toes, squeezing her ankles, pressing the bones together with my hands, almost hard enough to hurt, but not quite. She didn't appear to feel it. I dried them with the soft warm towel. Her toenails had chipped paint on them.

Where is your nail varnish?

What? The poet jerked as if I'd just woken her up.

Your nail varnish, remover, etc. Manicure stuff?

Why on earth would you want that?

Why do you think?

Bathroom cupboard. She went back to staring out of the window.

I used cotton wool to clean the chipped varnish from her nails. The smell of the remover was sharp, and inhaling it reminded me of the various things I'd smelled as a child and felt pulled to – petrol, markers, Tipp-Ex. The classics. I wondered if the kids that liked to smell that stuff are the same kids who go on to take drugs.

I rubbed lavender moisturiser into the poet's chapped skin, the smell of which made me think of Hetty. I chose a bright red. Slut red, whore red. The red of my throat after vodka, the red of winter berries and smeared lipstick and of Cosmopolitans drunk on hen dos. The red of the living, the breathing; the red of Blackpool and Soho and Broadway and Wall Street; the red of blood and of meat and of royalty. I painted her nails carefully. I kissed the soles of her feet and ran my tongue between her toes. You can't make someone live, but I was trying.

I had a meeting with my agent. A lunch meeting, in a Bistro Pierre, for some ungodly reason. I was early and ordered some of those little chorizo sausages doused with honey, and a large glass of red wine. It was raining outside again, in that way that feels completely endless, that makes you feel like the world is just drowning and will continue to drown until Britain floats away on the water like a piece of driftwood. I find it very difficult to achieve anything when it is raining like that, so I wasn't feeling positive about this meeting. It was sort of mutually agreed – she wanted to ask me about the collection I was working on, and I wanted to pitch another idea to her entirely. I say pitch, but I hadn't written anything. What I meant was I wanted to bounce my loose thoughts off her expertise and have her tell me it was a bad idea and be done with it. It would be a relief.

Rebecca was late. She always is. Not because she isn't organised, but because she knows people will wait for her and therefore factors it into her schedule. She has access to at least one extra hour per day that way. She's stolen time from everyone she meets. It's quite the skill and it impresses me. She has dyed black cropped hair with a severe straight fringe and wears those glasses with one round lens and one square lens. They're clearly expensive but look cheap because they are plastic. Nothing about Rebecca is cheap. She has been in the game for enough years to be completely jaded and to hate books, but she has a soft spot for me because she once had an affair with my father and because I flirt with her. I got my foot in the door using daddy's boot and I've kept it there with daddy's brown eyes.

By the time she'd arrived I'd finished my wine and ordered another. The little sausages came just as she sat down, and she swept one into her mouth before taking her coat off.

Delightful. I am sorry about the choice of venue darling, but Anthony's new restaurant is just around the corner, which is where I'll actually be eating lunch, this is a pre-lunch. I hope you can forgive me?

Of course, I can forgive you anything.

Well don't say that, you may live to regret it.

Never.

So how far have you got? she asked me, fanning herself with the menu.

Most of the way, actually. I've surprised myself.

And a theme? Is it filthy?

No. Well, there's sex in it, if that's what you mean. But then there's sex in everything. Even when there isn't. It's... there's more nature than you might be expecting from me.

Poems about nature? How very original.

Rebecca wrinkled her nose and ordered a miniature bottle of prosecco from a passing waitress.

Nothing is original, you know that. Besides, what do you care, it's not like poetry makes any money.

Young man, you are talented. Something you do will make you some money eventually. And I know you writer types. If you don't do the poetry, if you don't make the art, then you'll go mad, and I really don't have time for that.

The waitress came back with the prosecco and tried to take our order, but Rebecca waved her away.

So, what do you want to talk to me about?

It's something new. Not poetry, you'll be glad to hear. It's story of sorts. But it's true.

Well I never. Tell me more. Do we have a title?

It's called *Kingfisher*.

I drank a little more of my wine, and as I began talking, I realised I didn't need to have written my pitch down to have prepared one. By the time we'd finished talking Rebecca was late for her lunch and it had stopped raining.

Yellow. Yellow is the colour of life, don't you think? The colour of sunshine, or at least, human interpretations of sunshine. The colour of daffodils, and therefore of hope. The poet has a yellow leather handbag, a backpack really, and it has a matching yellow Moleskine notebook, where her ideas lie dormant like daffodil bulbs in the frozen earth. The handbag lies on the floor of the living room, occasionally dipped into for debit cards to pay for takeaways or online purchases. I keep filling the poet's flat with yellow, without asking her if that's what she wants. I buy bunches of forced sunflowers for every room. When I retrace the walks that we once took together, I see winter aconite pushing through the undergrowth and take it as a sign that she'll survive the season.

32.

I received an email from Michael. I suppose it had to happen eventually. It was quite familiar, not stinging of that unnatural formality that sometimes springs up after a relationship ends. He suggested a lunch, to 'discuss our situation'. I replied with a curt yes, and some potential days. His response was almost immediate, he could do the following day, at a bar we used to frequent when we were together.

That night I took a bath and washed my hair. I dithered at my wardrobe for a while, determined to decide what to wear before I went to sleep, to avoid any anxiety the following morning. It didn't work. I followed my writing routine, including the whiskey this time – cheap, sweet, American stuff. Now that I'd pitched the idea, I found the words came easily. I did not have to reach to catch them; they flowed over me, dragged me along with their urge to get into the world. I didn't think, at first, about the implications of what I was doing.

Chapter 1. By the River.

The bar was cold, a little studenty, no soft furnishings. When Michael and I had visited the place, we kept ourselves warm with beer and games of pool. Michael liked to watch the football and I liked the way the staff looked at us when I kissed him. I couldn't see him when I first entered, but after getting a drink I realised he was sitting on one of the battered leather sofas, his laptop open in front of him.

Hello, I said, and plonked myself down opposite. I was surprised at how normal it felt to see him.

You're here! he said, and I resisted the urge to make a comment about stating the obvious.

I am. How are you?

Oh, you know. He waved his arms around at the room as if that was supposed to signify something. I'm busy. The new gym keeps me on my toes. And we are opening a bar in the building. Lots going on.

You won't have to come to places like this anymore then.

He softened. I like places like this, he said.

So why are we here? I asked, sharper than I'd meant, but I was quickly discovering that it was painful to be in his presence and that the heavy-duty ignoring of my feelings and of reality that I'd been practising the past few months was only surface level. My previous life was slamming me in the face, and I'd forgotten quite how beautiful he was.

We are here because I have some news. Nicolás and I are getting married.

Of course you are. Jesus Michael you are predictable.

There is no need to be a bitch about this. He needs a visa, and I can get him one.

And you'll get the pretty little wife you always wanted. More obedient than me, is he? Does he do your washing?

Fucking hell.

Michael winced like he was in physical pain. I was embarrassed by my behaviour, but I didn't seem to be able to stop speaking like that.

Look, he said. Let's not make this more difficult than it needs to be. The visa application requires Nicolás and I to be living together. Currently, on paper, I live with you. It's time to decide what to do with the flat.

It was windy outside and really all I wanted was to be inside a bar like the one I'd just left, to drink alone until I found someone to drink with. But now I was outside doing that dramatic music video thing where you walk angrily into the wind without watching where you are going, all the while imagining your movie soundtrack, unless you've taken it further and are playing it in your headphones. *The aisles were endless and the piles of fruit began to fall towards us as we ran. My father and I would be crushed under the weight of one thousand oranges and I would be grateful.*

I was inconveniencing myself while Michael was in the bar I wanted to be in, and soon he would move back into the flat that I wanted to live in. I wasn't even sure that was true, but I felt obstinate and petulant and angry and hurt. Nobody likes to be left, even if it is the exact right thing to happen for both of you. I passed another bar, this one even more studenty, and then after a moment I doubled back and went inside.

My friend thinks you're gay.

Oh does she? Well, you should tell your friend that it's rude to assume people's sexuality.

I don't think you're gay.

So you're assuming too?

I bet her that you'd give me your number.

I can't let you lose a bet, can I?

The girl handed me her phone and I put my number in. I saved myself as 'gay guy at the bar' and handed it back. She smiled.

So, she's right?

I didn't say that.

The girl had ice blonde hair and her septum pierced. Her friend looked almost exactly the same as her except that her hair was black. They both wore big black boots, and I could see the straight guys in the bar eying them up. This might be fun. I reckoned they were about 22, which felt a bit gross because they were the same kind of age as the people I'd been teaching at the university, but I followed the blonde one over to her mate anyway.

The human brain doesn't finish developing until around age 26. By that logic anyone below 26 has a juvenile brain, and my principles told me that nobody with a fully developed brain should fuck anyone with a juvenile brain. But then, these girls were beautiful, and I didn't spend much time living by my principles. Perhaps it would be different now that I was in a relationship with a woman.

Can I buy you both a drink?

You can if you drink with us, said the one with the black hair. I called her Raven in my head, even though she told me her name was Katie. We're drinking this, she said, thrusting a pitcher of something green and luminous in my direction. It's called Eliminator.

Sounds perfect. I went back to the bar and ordered another jug. The bartender gave me three grubby pint glasses, but I made him swap them for those gin glasses shaped like balloons. If I was going to be eliminated with these girls, then I wanted to feel a little classier about it. The girls cheered when I came back and the other one told me her name was Esme, but I'd already renamed her Ice. I set about getting drunk with Ice and Raven in a student bar I'd never been to before and did my level best to stop thinking about Michael.

I was doing an extremely good job of not thinking about Michael, in fact. I was lucky that I'd found those girls, who were both witty and intelligent and deeply insecure in that way everyone is when they're 22. They worked hard to keep me entertained. They didn't need to, I found myself filled with hope in their presence. The light took on tones of yellow. They were so undamaged. From nice families who were helping them financially as they studied. Raven was doing a master's in economics and Ice was in the final year of her undergraduate degree. American Literature, which meant we had a lot to talk about. I always find it arousing talking to someone who loves books as much as I do. Except it's not quite love, is it? Because it hurts and I resent it. Maybe it is exactly love, then, but I think I need to find a new word. Whatever it was, I felt it strongly, sat on their battered sofa between them, back at their crumbling flat, as we shared lines of the pill Raven had just crushed up. Nothing makes you feel young and poor like snorting powdered ecstasy tablet. My face felt warm and supple, and I kept running a finger over my lips because the skin felt so soft and fresh.

We stayed on that sofa for hours, smoking and talking about who knows what. This was a kinder distraction than I'd been allowing myself in recent times, but it worked. They had gentle hands and checked that I was hydrated, made cups of sweet tea in the morning, and rolled cigarettes for me. They were silk and cashmere and fresh spider's web. I knew I was going to fuck at least one of them before I left their flat, but I wasn't pushing for it, really. I preferred this, this gentle company, the talk in soft tones. *My father was picking up endless oranges from the floor before discarding them. He could not find what he was looking for. I begged him to leave but he did not seem to hear me.*

To my surprise, Ice played us The Velvet Underground, and as Pale Blue Eyes eased its way from her Bluetooth speaker I wondered if it was a prerequisite for fucking me that women had to play that particular band. At least this song didn't have the added bloodshed of Nico's voice above the tender riffs, to disturb the peace I was beginning to feel.

When Ice and I finally wound up in bed together the whole thing made me want to cry. I wanted it to stop; she was so self-aware and made too much noise and was so exquisitely beautiful that I felt tears in my eyes but knew that we couldn't stop because it would hurt her. I thought about sitting on their sofa and talking quietly with them both for many weeks after that, but I never responded to the text messages I received from both girls. I was disgusted with myself for taking that peace from them.

33.

Rebecca called me.

We've had some interest.

We?

Me, you, the book. How quickly can you write me an actual proposal?

It depends, how in-depth do you need it to be?

Not particularly. But it needs to sing.

I can make it sing. What about chapters?

A couple, strong ones. How quick?

Give me a couple of days.

My hand shook as I ended the call. I was doing this then. I was actually doing this. There were so many people who would never forgive me.

You'll move in with me.

We were playing Cluedo, and the poet was going to win. She always won every game we played. It didn't feel quite so pointed with Cluedo, but I never wanted to play Scrabble with her again in my life.

Oh, don't say it like that. That's not what I'm saying. I'm just telling you what happened.

Well, yes, I know. But let's not kid ourselves. You'll move in here, surely. It just makes sense. You're here all the time anyway.

I'm not sure that's a good enough reason. Besides, Laurel will never go for it.

It's not her decision to make. Don't worry, I know you need your own space. You can take my old bedroom upstairs; the spare room is too small. And you don't need to pay rent, just get the food shopping in and do some of the house admin. It'd be good for me not to have to think about it.

You already don't think about it. I do all that stuff now.

Fine, make it official then.

Buying food was pointless because she didn't eat anything, but aside from that, she was right. I was here all the time. I looked at her thin face, her sharp cheekbones and tiny skull wavering on her thin neck. Her eyelids had a purplish tinge. She tilted her head to one side and looked back at me.

Professor Plum, in the library with the lead pipe.

I moved in very quickly after that. We didn't discuss it further, because the conversation made me very uncomfortable and because I knew that the poet wouldn't accept any money from me for living there. If I could just get my stuff in quickly, then we could just pretend I had always been there and maybe it would be less uncomfortable. It turned out I didn't own very much. Another uncomfortable truth. It was a good job she already had everything I needed. The furniture was Michael's and so was the coffee machine and the kettle and the TV. I owned every single book in the place except for two from a business course he'd started and never finished. He didn't need to finish; he already knew how to get a good deal from someone.

The poet gave me some sturdy cardboard boxes to use, and I packed up all my battered poetry books and pamphlets, annotated loose pages floating down to the floor like petals. I packed my various and nearly identical pairs of expensive jeans, my father's ashes, Hetty's ashes. I wrapped them both in bubble wrap and taped the lids of the urns closed. When I laid them in the box together, I realised it was the first time they'd been that close to one another since I was a small child. The thought made me smile, and in my new, bright room at the poet's house I placed them both on the windowsill, next to each other. What poetry it was, knowing how she'd hate it. I didn't know how my father would feel about it, but what did any of that matter now they were both gone. They could watch my mistakes and they could watch the birds in her garden, as we did every morning. I slept that night in her forest-coloured sheets on her tall, wide bed, just like the bed in her big, white house, and I remembered what it had been like when we lay there together. The following morning, I woke early and dragged the desk over to underneath the window and began to write again, fast, fluidly, like bleeding from a main artery.

Chapter 2. The Falcon.

I am bird-boy, I am changeling
I am becoming
that impossible thing.

Louis Bailey

34.

According to the ancient Greeks, kingfishers built their nests on a raft of fish bones and floated them on the Mediterranean Sea. To keep the kingfisher eggs safe, it was said that the gods always kept the seas calm and the winds low, while the eggs floated across the water. I wasn't sure what this had to do with anything, but I couldn't stop thinking about it. Kingfishers were said to incubate their eggs on the water for seven days before and seven days after the winter solstice. Halcyon days. We had not yet reached the winter solstice, and I felt that perhaps if the weather could just stay calm and fair, it would be a sign that the poet would survive. I have reduced myself to myths and legends.

The proposal was easy to write, once I got started. I had a clear idea of the narrative because it had all happened, was happening. I was in a unique position. A dying biography, if you like.

Jess's apartment is very white. The only colour in the kitchen is the fruit bowl, which contains pristine lemons and limes and nothing else. It looks like an aesthetic choice but really I know it's because she doesn't eat, except for biting a slice of lime in a gin and tonic. Except when she's out with me, of course, when we feast.

What are you looking at? She says, aggressively. Jess is always aggressive when she's in her own home. I can't decide if it's because she feels comfortable or vulnerable.

Your style choices.
And?
And you're an icon, as you know.
Good.

I just don't know where you keep your stuff.

She rolled her eyes at me, taking a bottle of vodka out of the freezer and beginning to mix us drinks. It's 11am which is early by her standards but I don't say anything. My role in our relationship is to remain reliably broken. She fixes me and I ensure I remain a mess for her to fix. It's the most functional relationship I've ever had. I can smell the brine from the olives she's using and the bleach in the cleaner that keeps the worktops so white.

I thought about what we were like when we first met. I was freshly out of the closet, and looking for any excuse to jump back in. She provided me with one almost immediately, smitten as she was. We had sex a couple of times, when I was drunk enough to let it happen without being too drunk to complete the deed. She shared her groceries with me and put my leftovers in her clean Tupperware. I let her. I let her assume this position of the woman in my life and I have never wanted it any other way. I don't often think about what she was like. She had Oxbridge confidence built in from childhood and yet was as vulnerable as a baby. She was a little overweight at the time, which she wore like a huge burden despite always being filled with a soft warmth that was beautiful to everyone. Many men liked her back then, but she dismissed them all in favour of the crumbs I gave her. Her blonde hair was very long and wispy like a child's. She wore oversized sweaters and jeans. She hid herself as she formed herself. The Jessica I know now is very different. She has eroded her curves into edges and demanded everything of the world but the love she deserves. I do not think of this often as I do not like to think of my hand in it.

Jessica offered to come with me to search for a seaside home for Hetty's ashes. She hadn't taken a holiday in about four years, and instead of jetting off somewhere beautiful she had chosen to come with me on a wintry tour of the British coastline. Odd behaviour, but I took her up on it.

I typed out instructions for the poet's care in great detail. When I handed them to Laurel, she looked so angry her eyes were barely open. I didn't have time for her ego; it was me that did all this stuff, me who knew what the poet ate and when, her medication schedule, what kept her entertained, how to make her body feel things again. Jessica and I were to set off on the Thursday, with me not due back at the office until the following Tuesday. I wrote a packing list while sat on the sofa next to the poet, who looked over my shoulder and made suggestions.

Will you take all of her? she asked.

Yes, I said. I want her gone. I want her far away from me. I hate that I can still feel her watching.

I got a little drunk that night and decided I would open the urn and tip Hetty into a large Tupperware, to allow for easy transit. There was something undignified about it that I enjoyed. I found some marigolds under the sink and put them on. The poet was asleep on the sofa, with *Have I Got News for You* blaring in the background. I left her there and placed the urn on the kitchen counter. I opened it up and discovered Hetty was in a clear plastic bag, the type you'd take a goldfish home in from the fair. Not that anyone won goldfish at fairs anymore. No matter how I tried I still could not picture her face.

Human ashes look just how you'd imagine them to look – somewhere between the contents of an ashtray and the surface of the moon.

When Thursday rolled around, I was incredibly tense. It was meant to be a holiday of sorts, but I couldn't get my shoulders to go down from around my ears. I massaged my temples, went back over the proposal draft I'd written. Hated it, suddenly, but sent it to Rebecca anyway. She replied so quickly it made me jump.

Good, she said. More.

Jessica arrived early with an immaculately packed suitcase, some sarcasm about how little packing I'd done and three takeaway coffees. I knew the poet wouldn't be able to drink hers, but I was so touched that Jessica brought it that I gave it to her anyway. I could see the poet was just as moved, and we both stared at each other for a few silent seconds as our eyes filled with tears that were obviously not so much about coffee as they were about humanity. I could smell medicine and plastic and the oak of the coffee table where I'd spilled a few drops of the poet's americano as I poured it into her mug. She held the mug to her face and inhaled the coffee and I could hear Jessica banging about in the kitchen doing that aggressive cleaning thing she sometimes does, which meant that she was trying not to cry too. We needed some music.

I switched on the radio and grabbed Jessica from the kitchen and waltzed her around the room to Rocket Man, which wouldn't usually work as a waltz but somehow did in that moment. I dipped Jess so that her blonde waves stroked the carpet and the poet laughed in delight. None of us said a word and nor did we need to. The poet mouthed along to the lyrics and closed her eyes. I followed Jessica back into the kitchen and saw she'd tided all the poet's scattered medication into a plastic box, with the weekly pillbox in front of it, the little door to Thursday already open and its contents scoffed. I moved my instructions for Laurel in front of it passive-aggressively.

Jessica pulled open the back door to let some air in (she is obsessed with making everyone cold all the time) and I caught sight of the bliss on the poet's face in the living room mirror, as she heard the screams of the birds outside. It was obvious, really. I ran to her.

You must go outside! I declared dramatically, like I was in amateur theatre.

What? she said, still holding the coffee to her face and smelling it.

You can't stay here in this house. You should come outside!

I swept the duvet off the poet's bed, took the coffee from her, and wrapped her in the duvet like a cigar. I carried her out to the garden and sat her at the table. She was so thin, I couldn't believe how sharp her shoulder blades looked, protruding from her back. Her tiny face was enraptured as she listened closely to the birds.

Robin, chaffinch, blue tit, goldcrest, dunnock, I heard her mumble to herself, counting on her ethereal fingers. I sat with her in silence, drinking my coffee.

35.

My father and I were at the market. We were trying to find my mother but she was hiding. Each corner we turned I could see a flash of blue as she ran ahead of us. She never wanted to be found. There is very little that is both blue and edible in the world. As we ran blue berries fell from the sky. I could hear his wings but I could not see them.

Dinas Cross – our first destination. The tiny place had no particular significance to me, except that we'd holidayed there once when I was a child. Perhaps that meant it had mattered to Hetty in some way. I had no memory of it at all, except for one photograph of the three of us together. My father had his hand on my shoulder and was looking right at the camera. My mother was looking into another world and I was looking at her. I must've been about eight years old. It was a long drive and I smoked too much, my arm dangling out of the window into the cold air. Jessica rolled her eyes and tutted but let me do it the whole way there.

We were staying in an Airbnb, close to the coast, as it was so much cheaper this time of year. The apartment was tiny, everything compact: small toaster, small kettle, small sofa, small shower. There was a photograph on one wall of a woman's eyes, close up, enormous, pixelated. I took it down and leant it against the wall to stop her staring. Jessica had the double room and I had the single. Because I am, of course, a gentleman.

What's the plan then? she asked, clomping out of her room having unpacked. I never unpack, but I knew she would have before she could consider going anywhere.

I hope you've brought some other shoes? I eyed her heeled boots.

I'll put on my farmer gear in a minute. I'm old money like you, remember? We know how to get muddy. I mean, how are you going to figure out if this is the place?

I don't know. Just go to the sea, I guess.

We changed into walking boots and old jeans. Jessica produced a grubby old Barbour jacket that I'd never have expected her to own. She kept in her gold earrings, and I realised they were one of the pairs that had belonged to Hetty. They looked good on Jess.

The wind was frigid and the sky bright. My nose numbed immediately, and I was glad of my leather gloves. The winter sun illuminated slices of thin cloud, scraped across the horizon like butter. We made our way down one of the many paths to the water's edge. I could smell salt and I felt absolutely nothing. I stood staring at the sea for a while. It was turquoise. It was beautiful, which didn't match with the occasion. Since she'd died, a lifetime of fear had begun to twist itself into anger. Into hate. When I tried to think about Hetty all I could see was a glimmering grey mass, a growth, malformed cells protecting me from the reality underneath. I couldn't smell her or imagine what her voice sounded like. If I focussed, I could picture her room at the care home, the wild gardens, her wheelchair in one corner, the shining brass handles on the drawers of her cabinets, but I could not picture my mother's face. Surely that meant this was not the place for her, but we had come all this way. I squeezed my eyes closed hoping to see something different when I opened them. But it was still turquoise. Jess stood watching me, her brow scrunched against the wind.

We are walking through the market and we break out into the sunshine. There is sand underneath my feet and I hold my father's hand in mine. I can feel his heavy wristwatch against my fingers as we walk. We are next to the sea and my eyes squint to take in the light and I can see my father's brown eyes. I can hear wings beating. There are stray dogs running around the brush but they are not thin and two play in the water together which is when I realise we are by the sea. I can see my mother laid out on a towel and she looks happy although she is underneath a hospital blanket and holds a bunch of yellow roses. I can smell lavender and my hand slips.

On the sand there is a seagull with one wing broken and twisted up backwards. The dogs see it and run in its direction and it tries to make for the safety of the water but its wing holds it down. The water is no longer safe. The sea throws it onto its back and it strains desperately to right itself. Bile rises in my throat and I am terrified and I let go of my father's hand. He walks over to the bird and lifts it gently from the waves and away from the dogs. It has a moment of safety but we both know it will die.

My mother is no longer on the shoreline and I cannot see her face when I reach out for my father's hand it has gone.

When I woke the following morning in the hard single bed, it was only 5am. I lay there as still as I possibly could and tried to imagine what it would be like to be dead. The problem is, of course, that when you're dead you can't do any imagining. In fact, death is the distinct lack of imagining, of thinking and feeling and trying to feel and trying not to feel. Hetty expended an enormous amount of energy on feeling hatred in her lifetime. Arguably it would have been less work for her to succumb to happiness, contentment, or even just boredom. But she worked harder than that. And I suppose I could not quantify the idea of her not being around because that particular strand of hatred she worked so hard on was so powerful that it must have left a residue. Perhaps I am that residue, or perhaps I can learn to love like my father. Perhaps that's what I am trying to prove with the poet. I wish that were true, in a way, for it would hurt less, but that's not what I'm doing. I am with the poet, and I am nursing the poet as she dies, because I am in love with her. It's a more mundane reason than I'd like. I am her witness and her saviour and I will write her story from her bedside.

I could hear the birds screaming their morning songs. *I'm alive, I'm alive,* they shouted together. *We made it through the night.* I can't recognise the calls of different birds the way the poet can, but I could hear the different tones of the seabirds compared to the birds in the poet's garden. I sat up and pulled back the cheap curtains, rested my chin on the windowsill and watched them flit about, occasionally landing on the roman stone wall at the bottom of the garden. I wanted to see a Sea Swallow, but I knew I was too late, that they wouldn't be here in this cold and wind. They would have flown away long before the winter equinox. Eventually I got up and made coffee, sat at the tiny table in the kitchen and began to write.

Chapter 3. Bridges.

36.

The tour guide was extraordinarily attractive. Really, it was too much. He completely destroyed Jessica's ability to construct a sentence and birthed a love of nature in the two middle aged women who shared the boat with us that was utterly unparalleled. I was too preoccupied to do much other than watch it play out in amusement. Especially as this man clearly loved dolphins more than he would ever love a woman.

The tours are usually closed this time of year, he told me, standing towards the front of the boat and exhibiting perfect balance against its movement. But your friend called us, and so did Joan and Joy over there, so we figured we'd take you out.

He put binoculars to his eyes and looked at the rocks above us.

We're out here every day anyway. Although I doubt very much that we will see anything.

I watched the perfect right-angle his elbow made as he raised his arm. I wanted to push him into the water. He was beautiful and for some reason it angered me.

The driver revved the engine and pulled the boat further out into the curve of the bay. I felt my body move back and forth with the swell of the water beneath us. Jessica put a blanket over both our laps and tried in vain to keep her hair out of her face. I pulled out my phone and took a photo of us. We looked like opposites, like negatives. She so fair and soft, me all olive and sharp edges. I took a hip flask from my pocket and drank. The tour guide frowned at me, but I offered it to him, and after a moment he took it from me, drank, then passed it to Jess. I felt like a child playing truant. I could see the other two women, Joan and Joy, out of the corner of my eye. They were both staring at the tour guide, whose name was Phineas, obviously, because he couldn't be called anything normal. He was hardly going to be a Kevin, was he.

I knew I was supposed to be looking at nature, but I cannot help always being most fascinated by people. I wanted to watch these women embarrass themselves in front of Phineas, I wanted to watch Jess flirt with him, watch her mind turn over the possibilities of being with this man, whose life was so different to hers. Humans will always do something horrible if you watch them for long enough. But it wasn't to be, not on this boat anyway, for the women began to gasp and point at the water, and I saw the dip and flicker of something moving underneath. Just as I saw it on their side, I noticed movement in the slick blackness and heavy foam that the boat cut through to my left. There were six dolphins in total, all charcoal and so much larger than I'd expected them to be. They kept pace with the boat for a few giddy moments and while they did it felt like the wind stopped; my frozen ears ached as if heating in front of a fire, and I couldn't hear the engine of the boat. I reached down to the jet water and let it soak my fingertips. And just like that, the beasts wished us a good winter and left.

I can't put her here, I said to Jess on our way back to the jetty. This is his place.

Don't you ever think that he's just everywhere?

Well, if that's the case, then where is she?

I don't know pet. I don't know.

We left that evening. When we got back to the little apartment, I made us coffee and cooked an oven pizza while Jess negotiated a refund for the following two nights, speaking loudly into her phone and thumping about packing at the same time. As we shared thin slices of Sainsburys margherita and I dipped mine into the mayonnaise I'd found in the fridge, she promised to accompany me to the next coastline the following week.

You're not alone, she told me, and although I knew this to be empirically true, I also felt more alone than I ever had. I needed to get back to the poet.

Laurel's face was completely still. It was as if she thought that human expression would soften her to me, and she needed to stay hard against her enemy. I was not her enemy, I am not anyone's enemy and all I truly wanted was to care for her friend with my very being, on a cellular level, but that was not how she saw it.

They want to move her to a hospice, she said.

I didn't respond at first, because I'd got so sick of looking at Laurel's face and waiting for her to begin talking that I'd begun staring out of the window and spotted a robin. He was perched on the back of one of the garden chairs, occasionally plucking something invisible from the metal and throwing it to the ground. He looked very busy.

I've been gone for two days and suddenly she wants to give up? Now you want to give up on her? She doesn't want to go to a hospice. Don't be ridiculous.

Laurel's cheeks had flushed but she kept her face very still.

She doesn't want to go; I don't want her to go. The doctors have said her level of care will need to be increased with this new medication. We have reached an impasse. They are now aiming for quality, rather than quantity, of life.

I turned my head and looked into the living room, where the poet slept with her head under her arm.

She looks fine to me, I said.

I got to my feet too fast and startled the robin outside, who flew away. I went out to the garden to smoke a cigarette. The birds shouted to me as I arrived. They knew who I was, even if Laurel did not.

Monopoly is my least favourite game. I don't like money, although I suppose the way I don't like money is reserved exclusively for those who have at least some of it. Property, capital, one's estate, were words I heard thrown about a lot as a child. My father was from a wealthy family, and Hetty wanted it. She had money of her own, but she wanted his. When I was young, she didn't really spend any of it, as far as I know. I think she was terrified of him leaving her, so she entangled herself so deeply into his affairs that he was never quite able to remove her. Not that he wanted to, not really, not until the very end. I think he thought he could make her happy. If he could just hold on long enough, one day she would break and surrender, and then their real lives could start.

I don't want to wait for my real life to start. My real life is right here, in front of this monopoly board, feeling my palms sweat with genuine fear as I began to lose. Hetty was never meant to be a mother. She didn't have the bone, if one exists. I was a way of ensuring that my father could never completely leave her. I was gestated in bad blood, nourished on stomach acid. When I was born, I became all too real. She lost so much blood that she needed a transfusion and was on bed rest for weeks after my birth. My father fed me, his was the skin-to-skin contact that sustained me, my tiny face pressed to his hairy chest as he bottle-fed me formula. I guess it's no wonder I can feel him everywhere and I have no idea where she is. Despite the fact that he died more than twenty years ago, it's been that way since I was born.

I don't want to go, said the poet, looking at me through narrowed eyes.

I assumed that was the case.

I think Laurel wants me to. I think she's frightened. I like it when you're around because you don't get frightened. Sometimes I wonder whether you feel anything at all.

I looked down at my clammy hands, my finger and thumb turning white as I gripped a little red plastic hotel. The edge cut into my finger. I didn't respond, because if the poet says I don't feel things, then I don't.

Do you remember the ice cream? I said instead.

The ice cream?

I remember hot sunshine and bare feet and mint chocolate chip ice cream. I remember you telling me about writing and about your life and I remember reading all the gravestones. Do you?

Of course I do. I wish I could walk like that again. I miss the water and the trees.

I could take you.

You couldn't. It's too far. I'm too weak. They want to put me in a hospice.

She said my name then, the word cutting into my skin. I've asked her many times not to say my name, and usually she respects it, except on the occasions I need her to the most. There was blood running down my face and I couldn't wipe it away because she'd told me that I don't feel things.

You might have to go, you know, I said. It might be better to be properly looked after. I don't know what I'm doing.

Not yet, she said, please not yet.

Okay, I replied. Whatever you want.

The poet was counting out monopoly money to pay herself. My hands had stopped shaking and I could see that she was crying tiny tears like the salt on the skin of a dolphin.

That night the poet asked to sleep in the forest bed with me upstairs. When I'd helped her take all her medication and clean her teeth and wash her face (for all her belongings were downstairs now, by the fire) I carried her upstairs. She told me that she wanted to feel something again and I obliged as best as I could. I undressed her and ran my fingertips across her thin back, traced the shapes of her sharp shoulder blades, pressed my lips to the pad of flesh remaining at the base of her spine. I massaged her feet and the curve of her fingertips, put my face to hers and kissed her dry, hard mouth. I was aroused but when she reached to touch me, I gently moved her hand away. I wrapped her in the green linen sheets and held her against me as we fell asleep.

The next day when I woke up, I left her there sleeping and walked before the dawn. I walked and walked in the winter half-light, wishing for the woods as my feet hit the tarmac. I passed a café at a nearby tube station. At first, I stood outside at the window, wishing I'd brought my cigarettes for something to do with my hands, but once I was still I began to feel the cold. I pushed open the steamy door to be greeted by a woman with a red sweaty face.

Americano, please, I said to her.

You look like you need it, she replied, turning to the large chrome coffee machine. Do you take milk and sugar?

Yes, I do need it, I need milk and sugar because the woman I love is going to die and there's nothing I can do about it.

Oh – said the woman, with her mouth open in a little circle. There was nothing else she could say to me, so her mouth stayed open like that as she turned back to the hulking machine and switched on the grinder. I could smell dew and burning and taste salt at the corners of my mouth. The woman handed me my coffee and passed me a gleaming croissant on a saucer, with a little glass jar of raspberry jam. It was warm and buttery and when I touched it with a fingertip it gave a little, as if melting.

You'll need one of these too then, she said. They're fresh out the oven.

Maybe I wasn't cut out for this. I wrote about the poet's thin skin and her tablets and the texture of her blankets. I wrote about the way the doctors and her friends looked at me. I wrote about her beginning to give me an allowance, about using it to buy myself new clothes and flowers for her, an endless cycle of fresh flowers she never commented upon. I imagined her screaming at me, calling me a thief. I wrote about the tubes in her arm and the look in her eye and how she was becoming translucent. I am a thief. But I was only taking what she could no longer use.

> *a pencil*
> *for a wing-bone*
> *from the secret notes*
> *I must tilt*

Lorine Niedecker

37.

Jessica had suggested I see a therapist, but I could not stomach the idea of spending £50 an hour just to tell a stranger that everyone around me kept dying. Telling an expensive stranger would not stop all the death floating into the air like ash, and it carried the risk of making me feel better about it all. You are not supposed to feel better about death. It is constant and reassuring in its weight, and without it, I feared I would just drift up into the sky like a scrap of burning paper.

The parking meter only took pound coins and neither Jess nor I had carried any cash since 2016. The wind was in our faces, the late morning sky blackening on the horizon, and all the tiny houses had their shutters closed. The coast looked exactly as I'd imagined it would, it looked like the oil paintings from the exhibition – splatters and swipes of black and green for the sea, churned brown for the beach. I could see the poet's patent shoes and wine-flushed cheeks and stained lips, but I still could not picture my own mother's face. Perhaps I could find Hetty on this coastline.

The windscreen of the car showed me that it had begun to rain, but it felt as if the air was just wet. I couldn't distinguish individual droplets. Perhaps we were walking through the sea, perhaps my retina had failed to flip everything right-side-up and I was standing on the clouds.

Jess and I sat in silence for a while. It seemed neither of us could face the next step. I thought about how grateful I was for her. Something I usually keep to myself.

Thank you, Jess, I said.

Oh don't be silly.

Just take it would you. You're the only thing keeping me going. I do love you, you know, whether you believe me or not.

I know you love me, in your way.

In my way?

You know what that means, don't pretend you don't.

I don't.

You don't love me in the way I want, was what she wanted to say. I did know that, I did know what she meant but if we vocalised it then the spell would break and I'd lose it all. So I stayed silent. I breathed slowly and watched the droplets on the window screen. Jess let the silence sit, too. There was a café up on the cliffs, with wooden benches outside. To my surprise, there was a sign swinging outside that signified that it was open, and the orange light in the window looked warm and enticing.

She doesn't love you pet. You know that, don't you?

I know. But it doesn't matter.

Jess bundled herself into a massive black scarf and stomped up the steps to the café. I'd hurt her again. I hurt everyone. The stone was splashed with green paint and speckled with seaweed. The café was indeed open, and we asked about the parking and were given pound coins after buying various things from the small and earnest man behind the counter. We ate haddock chowder and buttery teacakes and drank sweet tea as we watched the rain, now hammering against the window.

When we left the café and climbed back into the car, we were quiet again. We passed rows of bungalows, glowing blue like a carton of duck eggs. Ducks are evil. I imagined a future where I ended up here, retired, by the sea with my knees mutinying against me and a more conservative outlook on the world. No Michael to bring me coffees and no poet to brush my face with her feathers. I was sure Jessica was imagining a similar thing, except in her version she would be trying to smash that awful man into a palatable shape, squeeze him through the French doors of a duck-egg abode and have him bring her coffee in the mornings, as both their sets of knees also mutinied.

The annexe where we were staying was down a lane so narrow that the bushes brushed the sides of the car. It was the converted garage to a square and creamy-white cottage. The owners were incredibly nice and friendly when they met us with the keys. So much so that I had to pointedly explain the morbid reason for our visit just to get them to go away. There was a rushing stream passing the cottage with some white plastic chairs set up near the edge. It was far too cold to do so, but I sat in one and smoked while Jess went inside to unpack again. The sun had begun to sink into late afternoon light, that weakened winter light, and there was a reddish glow surrounding the camelia bushes. The couple who owned the annexe also owned some designer chickens, the kind with the fluffy feet, and they appeared to scratch around the base of my chair. They were tame enough to stroke. Chickens are not evil. Chickens can get depression and cows have best friends and pigs sing to their young, and I will never understand why sadistic scientists insist on finding out this information about the animals we are most cruel to. These chickens had a good life, a garden to scratch around in and food and shelter. Perhaps they are retiring here, like the imagined versions of myself and Jess I kept picturing.

It all felt so futile – fighting the weather just for me to finally admit that I couldn't feel Hetty here either. I left the ashes on the kitchen counter, and Jess and I walked around the town, empty and desolate out of season. I felt like I needed to heal something. I felt like I was absorbing the poet's energy as it leached from her body. She would be gone soon, and I would still be here. Perhaps if I told Jess about the book then she would feel better. Or perhaps she would see me for the snake that I am and no longer want to help me, no longer want to share food and long car journeys and packets of cheap sweets with me.

As the day wore on we began to relax. Jessica began to laugh at me again. She talked about this unworthy man she was seeing, and I did my best not to judge. We are all making compromises. It seemed to be a day of eating, as once our fullness from the little coastal café had subsided, we began looking for a chippy. We'd drunk the whiskey Jess had brought, smoked three joints between us and split a tab of acid and a single, battered-looking pill. I wondered if my teenage self would've thought me cool or terribly sad, wandering around Penzance gently high with a big-titted advertising executive hanging off my arm. I wasn't sure which way it would go. But the chemicals had begun to soften my edges and the rain had eased off, leaving in its wake a corner of afternoon sunshine that warmed our sodden jeans and made the pavements steam a little.

The water and the sky still looked like a painting, but this time I was painting it with my eyes as we walked and the pair of us kept falling into fits of giggles for no particular reason. Perhaps I could convince Jess to retire here with me, and we could move into a duck egg bungalow and let our knees crumble together and survive on fish and chips and psychedelics and laughter and neither of us would need to worry about being in love with anyone. It sounded a simple solution and certainly in the moment a wavering Jess agreed with my plan. We stumbled into a steamed-up chip shop with a bright pink painted frontage and Heart FM playing loudly in the background.

What'll it be then? said the thin man behind the counter. I felt weird about someone who worked in a chippy being thin. In Ireland they call them 'chippers' which made me feel good, like you had to be happy to go there 'cos it was fish Friday. The poet told me that.

Jess shoved me out of the way and reeled off our order. She paid and we went and sat down at one of the orange-pine tables at the window.

I took her hand. I know you don't understand it, I said, trying hard to look her in the eyes as the world rippled and warped around us.

Jessica, I said, I don't understand it either.

It was all gorgeous. The rain and the light and the cheap lino floor and the warmth of the radiator against my thigh. And my friend Jessica who loved me.

I love her. I have to be there. I am her witness.

38.

The coffee table in Kingfisher's flat was groaning with food. Too much for us to eat. But we were trying. Jess and I were eating on her behalf.

Sometimes I imagine myself settling down with a big manly man, said Jess. Not imagine, actually. I fantasise about it. It was all I could think about today.

She licked soy sauce from her fingers.

You know, like a carpenter or something, with big shoulders. I want him pretty but dumb, and I want him to spend all his money on me. Equality is all well and good, but we aren't actually equal, are we, and honestly, sometimes I just want to be someone's princess.

I replied through a spring roll – what you want is a modern-day Jesus figure. I could get on board with that.

Yeah, like Jesus but without all the God stuff. And with good tattoos and a van. He could do all the DIY and install under floor heating in the kitchen.

You're probably ovulating, said the poet, looking up from her crossword.

Pardon?

When women are ovulating, we are more likely to look for traditionally masculine traits in a partner. Then for the rest of the month we want dad bods and savings accounts, because then we might be pregnant and need security.

Is that science? Jessica held chicken satay in her hand as if it were a laser pointer.

Sure, why not. I read it somewhere.

Jess looked at her calendar on her phone. You know, I think

you're right. Well, just need to find me a Jesus type. Famously there's loads of those knocking about. Although I think I just want someone with calloused palms. David has really soft hands and it makes me a little bit sick. If I wanted to be touched with soft hands, I'd be fucking you instead.

She threw a prawn cracker at me.

David's a cunt anyway.

So are you.

Since the trip to Cornwall Jessica had stopped asking me what I was doing with the poet. I was glad. I needed them to get on. I did not find a home for Hetty in Cornwall. I was beginning to think I wouldn't find a home for her anywhere. We didn't even make it to the sea. Jess and I just got smashed in the Airbnb and then slept most of the following day. I'd have considered it a wasted trip had it not been so much fun. Perhaps that was my place with Jessica. I could take her back there in the summer and we could walk on the grass by the water and drink gin and juice from a plastic water bottle. We could take egg and cress sandwiches and sit on a blanket in the sunshine. Jess suited the sunshine, despite being from a country where there was none.

Someone from the *Guardian* wanted to interview the poet. This sort of thing wasn't unusual, except that this time they wanted to interview her because the cancer had come back. The poet's most recent book of essays had been a great commercial success, in as much as any book can be. She'd written at length about her first experience of cancer, so it stood to reason that people would be interested in her experience the second time around. They weren't to know how ill she was, I suppose would be the argument, but I was incandescent. My skin prickled with jealousy. She's mine. Her story is mine. It was the first time Laurel and I had agreed on anything. A young woman from the paper had approached the poet through her agent, and for whatever reason the agent had seen fit to pass the invitation on, rather than tell her where to go.

Deborah knows me well enough to know that I'd like to do the interview, said the poet, over a small cup of Thai coconut soup (it was a good day).

Well, I think it's bullshit. Who the fuck does this woman think she is?

She is a journalist; she doesn't think she's anything she's not. She's a young woman aggressively embarking on a writing career in an unfriendly atmosphere, and I have every intention of talking to her and respecting her questions. It's none of your business and it's none of Laurel's and I'm sick of you two henpecking me.

Jessica stayed silent and handed the poet a joint and a lighter. Those two were forming an alliance that I didn't particularly enjoy.

I've built a very successful career on being brutally honest about my lived experiences and I'm not about to stop now... So, you can stop looking at me like that.

Fine. Can I be there at least?

You can be there providing it's out of professional curiosity and nothing more. I want no mothering from you.

Mothering?

Yes, mothering.

That night I dreamed I was Hetty, and that I was drunk on vodka, and that I forced the poet to eat soap before she was interviewed and made her kneel on metal rods while she answered the journalist's questions. In my dream the poet had long hair that dragged on the floor and the journalist brushed it reverentially while she spoke. Bubbles were pouring out of the poet's mouth and onto her long hair. I woke in a sweat, tangled in the poet's linen sheets and I couldn't get back to sleep. When I crept downstairs for some water, I could hear that the poet was on the phone to someone telling them that she loved them. I'd never actually heard her say the words out loud before and I froze in perfect stillness to listen and ached for it to be me on the other end of the line. I only caught the end of the conversation, her goodbye to this mysterious person. I thought of our morning calls and of creeping out of bed and whispering down the phone like she was now, like our communication was some terrible sin that nobody else should hear.

39.

I spent the rest of that week in an anxious haze. I was back at work, and Jess and I wouldn't be heading off to any more coastlines any time soon, so suddenly all I had to focus on were the rapidly shrinking margins of my life. That and the writing, of course, and waiting to hear back from Rebecca.

The poet was distant with me, frustrated by my attitude, no doubt. My dream had rattled me, but I was more rattled by the fact that the poet had someone she said I love you to in the dark when I was at a safe distance. It could've been a relative, I suppose, but who, and why hadn't she mentioned it to me? I tried to write, but I was now so preoccupied by what the ending of the story would be that I found it hard to focus on the parts I already knew. My mind wanted to exist in the past, in Italian restaurants and in art galleries and on metal benches. Who was this person? What gender were they and were they older or younger than her? Did they have money and were they a poet too? A scientist? A doctor? Why was it that I knew about Kingfisher's medication and had accompanied her to her chemotherapy appointments but it was this person who was loved. I wanted to see them and smell them and understand who they were and why they existed.

I was furious. I ached and burned. I was consumed with a jealously that curdled in my stomach and distracted me from everything. How could I begrudge a dying woman the love of another? I shouldn't, shouldn't be able to, but it turned out that I could.

On the morning of the interview Michael called me and said he had some of my belongings that I'd left at the flat, and would I like to meet for a drink and to collect them. I felt confused and vulnerable, but I agreed to meet him that afternoon, after the poet's interview had been completed and after I had finished my care tasks for the day. Most of those tasks on that particular day consisted of making sure the poet looked as well as possible. I ran her a bath and filled it with oil of ylang-ylang and bubbles. I lit candles and played Liszt's Leibestraum No.3. I curated everything as if I had control. I washed her and helped her moisturise and choose clothes to wear that were both comfortable and elegant. I helped her wrap a piece of green silk around her head to conceal her naked scalp. I applied mascara to her remaining sparse lashes and when she could not find any blush to warm her translucent cheeks I used a pink lipstick, blending smears of it into a rosy hue.

Christmas was approaching, so I lit two cinnamon-scented candles and when I went outside to smoke, I doffed my cap to the robin. Robins on Christmas cards used to represent poor children. Christmas is a time of giving so perhaps if I worked especially hard then the poet would tell me she loved me as her gift. We could wake early and open presents in our pyjamas over crystal glasses of Buck's Fizz and shortcrust mince pies. It would smell of evergreen and of courage and of burning herbs.

The journalist arrived moments after I'd settled the poet at the dining table with a cup of fruit tea. I ushered her inside politely, taking her coat and hanging it in the hallway, and dutifully pottering off to the kitchen to make her a coffee. I used the machine, but then regretted it when I couldn't properly hear what they were saying over the sound of the beans grinding, the water heating and the milk steaming. But I could tell from her tone that the journalist was being complimentary. I heard whispers of the poet's book titles, particular essays. It was clear that the journalist was a fan of hers. I relaxed a little.

When I took her coffee in to her, the journalist smiled at me, and I saw she had an open face. A beautiful face. She had a severe straight fringe that cut across this face and a Welsh first name. For some reason I found that comforting and I retreated back into the kitchen. I made myself a black coffee and sat at the breakfast bar from where I could see the poet. She looked more alive than she had in days, but not because of the makeup I'd applied. The journalist had not even pulled out a notebook or a recording device; they just talked in soft tones. I was relieved to realise that I could still hear them.

So, I'd like to begin with the more logistical stuff, if you can bear it, said the journalist, finally pulling a notebook from her bag.

I knew it would be a notebook. The poet inspires the tactile and the analogue. Crisp paper. Soft leather.

Of course, said the poet, begin wherever you like.

When were you first diagnosed with breast cancer?

Well, and I've written about this extensively, as a coping mechanism no doubt, it was just before my forty-eighth birthday. I did my best to be proactive and opted for a bilateral mastectomy. I was given the option to have just the one breast removed, or to try and preserve the nipple and some of the breast tissue, but I declined.

And you've also chosen not to have reconstructive surgery, is that correct?

It is. I have always been very slight, I had very little breast tissue to speak of anyway. And having never wanted children, I had no use for nipples. Their aesthetic or their sensation didn't feel important, what felt important was not dying.

You wrote in your most recent essay collection about romancing your new body. Could you talk a little bit about what that means?

Of course. I began to get regular massages. I saw a counsellor. I also chose to seek the services of a sex worker. Something I know some people saw as controversial. She was a woman, because I wasn't comfortable with the physical dynamic with a man. And most of the male sex workers I found who took female clients were too masculine for me. I wanted femininity and delicacy. I wanted someone who would truly understand my purpose. She provided some of the massages, but we also worked on sensual touch together. It turned out to be quite the creative collaboration. She became a close friend. She is very skilled in her profession.

Did it bother you that some people thought this problematic?

Not really. If I spent time thinking about what others thought of me then I'd never get anything done. I paid her extremely well for her services and she was the one to decide on how our sessions would work. I trusted her - trust her - implicitly.

Were there any other methods you used?

I hate to sound like a terrible old hippie, but outdoor swimming helped a lot. Just being outside was important. I began wearing loose clothes, no underwear. Walking barefoot in the woods. Perhaps I am a terrible old hippie. But it worked. I reconnected with my body; I began to venerate my new shape. I traced the outline of my scar every night before I went to sleep, and every day when I woke up. I drew it, modelled for artists to paint it. I have the images framed in my house.

And, perhaps most importantly, I took many lovers. I still do. I allow people to pleasure me in a way I never did before my cancer. And now I've been diagnosed again, and likely this time terminally, I have taken that practice further. I allow people to serve me.

40.

I put my hand on the back of his head. I took handfuls of his hair. I pulled and pinched his earlobes the way he liked. I'm pretty sure I am better at giving head than Michael is. Or he is better at receiving it, I'm not sure which. Either way, it was exactly what I needed. To be given something.

I could tell you how we ended up there, back at the apartment I'd shared with him, the apartment I'd lived in alone not so long ago, but you don't need to hear it. You know how it goes. It doesn't matter how I got here. It doesn't matter that I'm here. I don't like to think of myself as heartbroken. Lustbroken, perhaps. Egobroken. Sex with Michael was my Kintsugi. I was trying to glue myself back together.

I was having trouble sleeping. The skin was cracking at the corners of my mouth. My cuticles bled from my relentless teething of them, and grey trenches formed beneath my eyes. My hair felt thin and lank, and I began to scrape it back off my face, tying it in a knot at the back of my head. For a few days after the poet's interview, I stayed at the flat with Michael, in our old bed. Nicolás was in Mexico, visiting family. I let Michael fuck me every night. I wanted him to hurt me, but he was relentlessly gentle. Unremittingly tender. Interminably kind.

I ate the flaccid eggs Michael prepared for me before he went to work. He seemed busier now, more animated. I don't know why I was so surprised. Or hurt, for that matter. The poet had known about Michael from the beginning of our relationship and hadn't been phased. Why would it be any different for her. I was the last person she would expect to be bothered by something like this. But I was bothered. I could think of nothing else. Was the woman she wrote about who she'd been on the phone to? Or was that someone else? Someone else she allowed to serve her. That's what I was, then. A servant. I don't know why I'd ever thought about love. I was the lover. The giver. Never the recipient. I was irritated, hurt, but it quelled some of the doubts that had been surfacing about the book. She was taking what she wanted from me. I would do the same.

I behaved differently in our old flat. Nicolás' belongings were here now, the place felt warmer. There was a red throw across Michael's severe grey sofa. The bathroom was cleaner and there were scented candles around the bath. The wardrobe contained his clothes, which smelled sweet, like warm milk. I tried to write again, but this time while drinking loose leaf earl grey and wrapping the red throw around my shoulders. My words were crueller while I was there. I was careful to have cleaned and made food before Michael came home, because I wanted to feel useful. I didn't want to have to go back to the poet just yet. Jessica phoned me.

She wants to know where you are –

I don't want to say.

She's had to get Laurel round to help her while I'm at work.

Laurel will love that.

Can't I know where you are?

You'll guess if you think about it.

Stop playing games.

I'm not. I'm too tired to play games. It's winter, I'm hibernating.

She's having the tree delivered tomorrow. I thought we could all be there to decorate it. I'll make mulled cider.

Like we're a happy family? She can't drink.

She can have apple juice. Don't be pedantic.

I'm being careful.

You're never careful.

Come home.

It's not my home.

Christmas was a good time for me as a child. My father had time off work, and every other year he would fly his mother over from Italy to spend the season with us. Hetty would retire to her room to drink alone, and my father would read the fat crime novels he didn't have the time for the rest of the year. I spent the time in the kitchen with my nonna as she prepared all the food.

Noni trusted me to use the big knife to chop vegetables, and to scrub potatoes with a nail brush until my little hands turned red from the cold water. I knew if I completed these tasks to her satisfaction, I would be allowed to help her roll the pasta for lobster ravioli, and, best of all, lick the bowl when she made chocolate truffles. She would make coffee for my father and allow me to carry it carefully to him, my tongue between my teeth in concentration. Noni was the first adult to teach me about secrets. She'd let me suck on the slice of lemon from her gin and tonics, and when I turned ten, she began to allow me a drag on her Silk Cut cigarette that she smoked by the back door.

I remember my father in flashes of tactility. His hand when he took the coffee from me, thick knuckles, black hairs. The expensive watch hanging weightily on his wrist. His lips when they brushed my forehead. I can smell Old Spice and cigars, feel the cashmere of his sweaters between my fingertips. Most of all, of course, I have his voice. It was the last thing left to me, when Hetty took me away. Some mornings I wake in a terrified sweat, thinking I've lost the sound of him, but it always comes back. *When I think of my father I can hear wings and smell orange rind. I know I must run but I cannot tell which direction.*

On the last Christmas I had with him Noni cooked a goose. It was heavy and awkward, and she was getting older and couldn't manage, so my father helped her. He put the tray in the oven and took over the job of basting it for her. He sat her in his armchair and brought her a gin and tonic and she fell asleep. My father and I finished cooking the Christmas dinner together, as he drank brandy and told me ever more exciting tales of his days in the RAF. It was the best Christmas dinner I'd ever had, despite Noni being a far better cook. We ate it at the kitchen table and my father told me that I was a man now, and that I had to look after my mother, even when she was being difficult. He smiled knowingly when he said 'difficult', as if it were some specific state, like having a fever. I knew what he meant but I remember still feeling confused. Hetty was always difficult. Perhaps I'd be better off flushing her ashes down the toilet. They'd reach the sea eventually.

It's like this, mother, you must go now.
Just imagine it was you instead of him.
Just imagine it was me instead of her.

When I moved out of Michael's apartment I'd left in a panic and forgotten our old kitchen table, with the coffee rings from my father. Nicolás had covered it in a white cloth. It seemed I'd come back here for a reason other than misplaced comfort for a bruised ego.

Nicolás is home tomorrow, Michael said as he passed me a glass of red.

I know. I'll leave tonight.

It's been good to have you back.

It's been good to be back. But I can't stay.

I know, I was going to say the same.

We can't do this again.

I know.

I have to take the table, Michael.

Of course. Let me help you.

Later that day, when I'd packed the few random items I'd missed into my rucksack, Michael kissed me in the hallway. It was soft and sweet and soothing, and I understood that we'd healed what was torn between us. I wouldn't see him again; I was sure this time. He helped me carry the table down the stairs and even drove me to the poet's apartment with the table in the back of his car and the seats down. We didn't talk on the drive, but we did smile at each other when we caught eyes.

I could see from outside that the tree had arrived. Jessica was in the living room with her back to the window, fighting with fairy lights. They'd started without me. I'm not quite sure why, but I rang the doorbell. Perhaps I thought those few days away meant that I didn't live there anymore. The poet answered the door wearing a blue silk kimono and sheepskin slippers.

What are you doing out here, you fucking idiot? she said, throwing the door open wide. We need you to put the star on the tree, neither of us can reach.

Good to see you too.

I carried the table into the hallway without an explanation and went straight to the kitchen. As promised, there was a pot of hot cider on the hob. I helped myself to a mug, went into the front room and took the lights from Jessica. Between us we untangled them and wrapped the tree. Jess handed me the golden star for the top. It was made of thin, hammered metal, and I cut my finger on one of the points. The poet licked the bead of blood away, and carefully wrapped it in a plaster.

41.

I have had enough of death, yet I have already begun to mourn her. We managed to spend Christmas in the flat together before it became necessary to move the poet to a hospice. I am a bad carer. I do not understand enough about medications and rest, and I cannot be relied on if she were to crash, if her tiny body were to suddenly lurch a step closer to death rather than continue its gentle stumble. Before she was moved, I was given access to her room. I hung the painting of the arctic tern above the toilet in her ensuite, trying to ignore the safety bars, the red alarm cord hanging down to the floor. I wanted to pull it, to hear it buzz, to have people rush to my aid.

I made the tall bed with linen sheets from the poet's own linen cupboard. I placed a vase of forced sunflowers by her bedside. The colour of hope. I filled a bowl with cherries that glistened from the water I ran over them, washing away any impurities. The poet cannot ingest impurities unless a doctor injects them directly into her veins. But there was less of that, now. There was morphine, and often she could no longer answer the quiz questions when I asked them.

Days oozed into weeks. When I wasn't working I sat at her bedside, recording everything. Jessica came by in the evenings, so that I could go down to the cafeteria and get something to eat. Most nights she stayed with me there until late, but sometimes she went straight home. She often drove me back to the poet's flat around ten at night, and I'd sit silently in her obnoxious car, not wanting to go inside and be there alone.

I left the Christmas tree where it was, a monument to our last freedoms together. The hessian carpet was thick with green needles. I woke with the dawn and stood in the garden, smoking, and greeting the birds. Robin, chaffinch, blue tit, goldcrest, dunnock, I'd whisper to myself. A mantra. A prayer. I wrote her story.

Chapter 4, The Gallery.

Chapter 5, The Kiss.

Chapter 6, Admission.

Chapter 7, Sunday Morning.

Rebecca had a publisher interested. Then another. They could fight for it.

42.

Did you ever read that book?

Kingfisher was sat in the small green armchair next to the bed. Her cheeks were flushed, and she looked so beautiful that I almost didn't notice the tubes in her nose.

What book?

The only book I've ever lent you, obviously.

I didn't want to say, but the truth was that I'd started it and found it impenetrable. It was the poet's favourite author, so I could hardly say that I didn't like it.

You didn't like it? she said.

Fuck. I'm sorry, I said. I did try.

That's okay. You're not ready for it yet.

I'll try again.

You should. But not yet. Now what's the next question – I've got about ten minutes before my head is completely fucked again.

Which Mexican artist produced works entitled *The Broken Column* and *Diego and I?*

That's far too easy. Where did you find this fucking quiz? Try harder.

I did try harder. For the first time in my whole life, I made it my mission to become a good person. I put other people before myself. I cleaned Jessica's house like she'd so often cleaned mine. I collected her dry cleaning and did food shopping for her. I bought her roses. I brought everyone I knew fresh flowers and loaves of homemade bread. I tried hard at work, applied earnestly for other writing fellowships, for jobs where I could be of use to others. I stayed up late at night and woke early in the morning and I finished my first full collection of poetry. I continued to write her story. My story. I didn't have any family to care for, not of the blood kind, so I cared for Jess and the poet with everything I had.

For the most part, I think they found me a pleasant irritation. But it was such a glorious change from being a disappointment that I drank it in like fresh, cool water.

My father used to take me fishing.

The poet said this one afternoon, apropos of nothing, as she sat in that green armchair. Someone who worked at the hospice had given her an origami kit, and her thin fingers worked sheets of coloured paper into the shapes of animals. I had not yet summoned the courage to ask her where the newspaper swan I'd given her had gone.

He did? So did mine. I didn't like it. Too messy.

He would bait the hook for me. I was quite the girly girl as a teen. Long nails. She fluttered her fingers at me. I didn't want to touch any of it. The other men often laughed at him. She looked dreamily out of the window.

I caught a lot of fish though. More than any of them.

She went back to carefully folding the paper. The sheet she held had a pearlescent effect, like the inside of a shell.

Our communication had become like this. She didn't talk much, instead retreating inward. She completed small tasks with her hands – she would still play cards and board games with me, but now she'd silently lay down her winning hand before drifting off into a trance-like state until I handed her fresh cards. I became her translator. I spoke to the kind people, mostly women, who came to look after her. I decoded her moods and her silences, explained why certain foods remained on her plate after her tiny meals, suggested different things they might like to get in to appease her waning tastes. It was a very expensive place, and they were more than happy to oblige.

From the outside it might seem like the poet was melting away, like the life was beginning to drain from her, but if I watched carefully enough, I could see that something else was happening. Her behaviour was restorative. She was gathering the little energy she had left and concentrating it in her mind. She was writing. Even when the pain was bad and she would lie there with eyelids half closed, her breathing becoming so shallow I would almost get up to find a mirror, she was writing.

43.

Jessica took me out for a big fancy dinner. It was something we'd not done in a long while. We had become something different. I no longer entertained her in the same way. I think we both felt old, although we knew we weren't. I think grief makes you feel old on the inside. You've seen what the end looks like, which makes it harder to be jolly and hopeful about the middle parts of life, no matter how much collagen remains in your cheeks and how much colour in your hair.

It was an Asian fusion restaurant. The cocktails looked like pieces of art and we drank many of them. Jessica had received a bonus – somehow, she was still being remarkable at her job while simultaneously carrying me through my empty evenings. She is a miracle. She is the human embodiment of a daffodil. Strong and bright and first to arrive.

We ate Korean barbeque, which I'd not had before, and, in this restaurant at least, meant cooking your own food. The centre of the glossy black table lifted off to reveal a hotplate, and with choreographed precision three waiters appeared with plates of crisp greens, pak choi and celery and stuff I didn't recognise; dishes of raw salmon cut in frivolously thick slices; and best of all a pile of fillet slivers, oiled and salted and sliding off one another on their bed of leaves and edible flowers. It was a landscape of food, and the sensuality involved in the sizzle of it cooking, in the concentration I required to use chopsticks, and the pure, immaculate beauty of it all made me feel connected to my body again in a way I hadn't felt for weeks. We ate and drank like Renaissance royalty. We barely talked, having said everything there was to say to one another in our near daily car rides home. It was an extravagant silence. My brain quieted.

About halfway through our feast, a waiter arrived with a bottle of Urakasumi sake. He explained it had been sent to us with compliments from the Awful Man. The waiter told us that the word 'urakasumi' meant 'misty bay', a reference to the location where this sake was made. Jessica was embarrassed but pleased and I made a point of googling the sake and making some terrible jokes about how tiny his cock must be if he was spending that much money. It was almost like old times, except that I took a taxi to the hospice when we had finished our dinner.

I was wavy and sick with the taste of steak. Myoglobin. My muscles had no oxygen. I don't think I was supposed to be allowed up to the poet's room at this time of night, but somehow my arrival had timed itself perfectly with staff tea breaks, or possibly shift handovers, because the front desk was empty, and I made my way to the lifts unchallenged. I walked slowly along the corridor. The moon was bright, and the minimal space was lit with its white light. I stepped slowly, partly because I was quite drunk and didn't want to wake anyone, but also partly because now I was here, I didn't actually want to go to her room. Now I was here, and everything was lit with moonlight I realised I might be able to truly see how ill she was. Would there be machines beeping and would there be medications laid out on the side waiting for consumption? Would she be breathing so I could hear her, or would she be silent? Would I be able to tell whether she was alive? Part of me wondered whether I had sought her out just to lose her.

When I reached her room, I didn't go in. I sat on the floor outside her door, and I cried the tears I knew I wouldn't be able to bring forth once she was gone. I cried tears for the poet and through her I cried tears for my mother and for my father. I must have fallen asleep right there in the corridor, for I was woken when the sun took over from the moon, by a nurse arriving to check on

Kingfisher. She took me wordlessly to the staff room and made me a cup of coffee with both milk and sugar, and gave me tissues to wipe my face. How many kind strangers there are, for all of us, and how often they know the value of silence and soft hands.

*We can make do with so little, just the hint
of warmth, the slanted light.*

Molly Fisk

44.

I slept all day that Sunday, after my dinner with Jessica, after my night on the floor of that white corridor. I didn't go back to see the poet that day, and I did not hear anything from her. On the Monday I was at the office and melted through the hours as if I were not really there. Afterward I drove to the hospice and there she was in that green armchair. I do not know if she realised I had skipped a day, or if she had heard me outside her room that night.

The hospice has a garden. It has high red brick walls around it, the bricks mottled in different tones. There were enough trees that in areas it felt like a purer version of woodland than it was. If you squinted, you could imagine the building was gone. But it wasn't, and pretty though it was, its shadow was enough to ruin the illusion. The garden was beautiful, in a wild way. Not unlike the gardens where Hetty had lived. I began to take Kingfisher out in it. It had wheelchair-friendly paths that I would walk her down so that she could smell the air and hear the birds. She didn't really talk when I did this, I think because she was too overcome with emotion. I was not the only one grieving her before she was gone.

It's not enough, she would say to me as I helped her into her chair.

It's just not enough.

Jess had offered to go away with me again. I was still confused as to her motivation, or mine for that matter, but I accepted. I was still compelled to find an ending, of sorts, having discovered that death is not an ending at all, but the beginning of something else entirely. The next destination on my ashes pilgrimage would be Holkham beach, in Norfolk. It would be bitterly cold. I was hopeful. It was near where Hetty's mother was from, my grandmother, a formidable and once rich woman who died very poor. I was struggling with how to conceptualise an entire world into which to place the remains of my mother, so it felt helpful to hang our choice onto something. But on the morning that Jessica and I were due to leave we received a call from the hospice. The poet was in a bad way. She had asked for both of us.

When we arrived, she was asleep. We were taken into a small room and told that her breathing had been much more laboured that day. That she'd been losing consciousness, but that she'd been very insistent about us being there. I went and sat by her bedside while Jessica went to get us coffees. Occasionally the poet's chest would jump slightly as she breathed. Her skin was soft and downy to the touch, like a fresh hatchling. Jessica had a bed made up in her room. We slept in it together, my face pressed into her shoulder. When I woke up Jessica was gone, and the poet was awake.

Hello, she said, and her eyes looked bright and black. Unblinking.

Hi. You're up.

I am. I have a small window of energy. Will you take me outside?

That's what I'm here for.

The January air was quite gentle with us when we ventured out of the automatic doors and into the garden. It was a frosty morning, the grass held stiffened in an icy spasm. But the air was mild. Our breath fogged in front of our faces, and I felt a certain relief at being able to see the poet's breath so clearly. She felt strong that day, that much was clear. Her spindly neck held her head high, her pale and naked scalp shielded by a chenille hat, purchased by Jessica, who is always concerned with textures. The poet deserved softness, I agreed. I felt that she was using up some of the energy she'd worked so hard on conserving. I wished she wouldn't, but I could not say that.

We followed the wide paths as they wove their way around the space in an aesthetically pleasing manner. Someone clever had designed this space. Someone who understood the rhythms of nature, who understood shapes and textures. Someone who understood what branches would be empty in winter and had factored their delicate shapes into the thicker textures of the evergreens, the huge ferns now blinking with white ice, but still pretending at a warmer clime. The birds screamed. They don't sing, I am certain. They scream out to be heard. Not to be forgotten.

I haven't much time left, have I?

So they say. But they could be wrong.

They could be. But they won't be.

I need to come out here every day. Will you make sure they take me?

Of course.

Stop saying 'of course' like this is normal. You can cry, you know. Or shout. Or say something that makes me believe you are a real person. You're going to watch me die.

I know.

Doesn't it make you angry?

I don't get angry much. I get empty. It's making me empty.

Good. That's better than nothing.

—

I want to die out here. Will you bring me outside so I can die under the trees?

I will. I promise.

I'd begun, I think, to accustom myself to my role as servant. It was simpler, not to torture myself with the possibilities of anything more. While sat at her bedside I flicked through the apps. I made dick appointments to attend once I left the hospice for the night, and forced myself to call them that. I courted crassness. It felt safe. I told her about them, a little, and I made her laugh. I did everything I could not to think about the person on the other end of that phone call, and I never asked her. I imagined what their skin might look like. Was it dark or pale, did their hair curl like hers or was it straight like mine. Did this woman, for I'd convinced myself it was a woman, did she know about theatre? Had she taken the poet to the theatre before she became too ill? Or was she an ornithologist? Did she teach the poet about all the birds she loved so much, teach her about flight paths and bird calls and mating patterns?

After much discussion, mostly between Jessica and Kingfisher, it was decided that Jess and I would take our trip to the beach after all. The poet was furious at the suggestion of us not going: one day of bad breathing did not mean she would kick it immediately. She was still conscious, and anyway she was the one who was dying so she got to choose what we did. I was shocked by how much fury she had left in her, but then, perhaps fury is exactly what one would feel. Jessica cried a lot, and even shouted at her at one point. I stayed silent. Those two had formed a friendship right under my nose. But we were to go. The staff at the hospice had our numbers and would call if anything changed. We would only be gone two days. I packed the car reluctantly.

This time, Jess drove. I looked out of the window. I opened my laptop, wrote a few words, closed it again. I flicked through radio stations until Jessica threatened to throw me out of the window. We played I Spy, tried to imagine what people were doing in other cars, made judgements about other people's driving. When we stopped at a service station I burst into tears, and we stood in the carpark as I heaved heavy sobs into Jessica's chest, my feet pressed into the grey grass of the verge, my back hunched. Snot and tears and spit streamed down my face and with each cry my chest heaved as if I would not be able to catch my breath. I felt as if someone had cut me chin to crotch. Everything was falling out. She'd said my name again. It was always worse when she said my name. Jessica held me for as long as it took, and I wiped my face with rough napkins from Costa. We got back on the road without a word.

When we arrived at our hotel, we were both completely sapped of energy. We needed to hibernate. We leaned on the reception desk as if it would replace our legs. The woman who checked us in had an orange foundation tideline on her neck and lipstick on her teeth. I wanted to wash her face. To dunk her head in a bucket of water.

A twin room, you say? she said, looking at us suspiciously. Quite what she thought was going on I do not know.

Just look at the fucking booking and give us the key, will you?

Jessica never spoke to people like that.

I walked away. My phone buzzed in my pocket. Rebecca.

Yes?

What the fuck do you mean, yes? *Hello, how are you?*

Sorry. I'm tired. It's been a lot recently.

I'm calling with good news, you little shit. It's sold.

To who?

Your favourite.

How much?

Better than we thought.

How long?

Get the fuck on with it.

Wow.

Kisses, she said, and hung up the phone.

Jess and I made our way down the central-heated corridor in silence. It smelled like a window had never been opened. Stale, hot, like climbing inside an old oven dish. We both dropped our bags; this time Jessica did not unpack. She closed the curtains and we crawled under the sheets in our clothes. I could hear her breathing change to the slower rhythms of sleep in just a few short minutes. It felt like I was awake for hours. I took the Tupperware containing Hetty out of my bag and placed it on the bedside table. I eventually fell asleep with the little pile of ashes the only thing in my eyeline. If I closed one eye, I could believe I was in a desert. I could believe I was lying on the moon.

45.

When I woke I called the number for Hetty's old care home, and didn't realise what I'd done until the receptionist answered. I thought about the ivy on the walls and the clean stripes of the lawn until she hung up on me, which didn't take long. I was haunted by carpets and ice cream and music and Thai food.

That night we ordered room service. I took a bath and changed into the white fluffy hotel robe. Jessica ate profiteroles and I had chocolate fudge cake. We pushed the beds together and rented movies to watch. Jessica cracked a bottle of New Zealand sauvignon blanc; I drank whiskey, as I always do.

I've been reading her books, said Jess, her mouth thick with cream.
I didn't know you read.
Fuck off. I'm trying to be sincere.
Okay, okay. I'm sorry. Bad taste. What do you think of them?
She really is magnificent, isn't she?
She is.
I wish I'd never started. It makes it so much sadder.

I fell asleep again. I dreamed of my father. Why do I always dream of my father? It was his birthday and he was older than I'd ever seen him. We ate together, and when we'd finished he handed me a cigar. When I lit it, it burst into flames and I dropped it on the floor. I could hear wings, but then I can always hear wings. The thick carpet caught alight and in the distance I thought I could see Hetty sinking, but I couldn't make out her face. When I woke Jess had the TV on silently, some black and white film. I leant my head on her shoulder and wept.

We used to watch the cricket together.
Pardon?
Me and Hetty.
I fingered the corner of the Tupperware that held the ashes. I had an urge to open it and poke my finger in, but I didn't.
She used to get so excited. I don't know how... even the players don't get that excited about cricket. But she loved it.
Jess took my hand and squeezed.
She'd call me when I was at uni. Tell me all about it. I used to put her on speakerphone while I got dressed or whatever. I liked listening to her voice when she was like that. It was as though we'd finally found a language. I didn't really speak it, but I liked the sounds. The cadence of it all.
That's nice. I think that's the nicest thing you've told me about her.
What, that she liked cricket? Speaks volumes.
Still. Better than nothing.
Jess sighed and tipped her wine glass back to get the final dregs.
She's the reason I'm like this.
No, she's not. You are.

46.

The beach was blistering cold, the surface crushed flint, the air filled with knives. The light was shy, our coats not enough. Jess linked my arm, and we fought our way closer to the sea. This really could be the moon, were it not for the black water licking at our edges. I could not see the beginning or the end of the coast. We made it down the rocky path, all that was between us and the sand were some stone steps. I slipped on the final few and fell, Jessica rushing down behind me. The base of my spine smacked into the bottom step, the hand that grabbed at the handrail to stop my fall was bleeding. On closer inspection I saw that most of the skin was missing from my palm, and it was littered with splinters from the wooden rail. There was one wide gash down the middle, framed with grazes.

I was laughing even as tears formed again in my eyes. Jessica sat on the step next to me and in the blast of the wind she carefully removed chips of wood with her long nails. My palm began to fill with blood as if I was trying to carry it somewhere, so I tipped it out onto the sand and staunched it with a dirty tissue from my pocket.

Do you want to go back?

No. I think this might be the place.

We walked into the wind. At the water's edge I took off my boots and socks and left them on the grey shingle, walking into the cold up to my ankles while Jess laughed maniacally at me from the shoreline. I shook so violently that my shoulders bounced, and my teeth smashed together. I washed my hand in the salty water only for blood to spring forth again. I took the Tupperware from my jacket pocket and held it with shaking fingertips. I opened the lid and tipped the ashes into the water, but the wind took them sideways, and my skinned palm went from red to black.

47.

I'd had a long, hot bath. My fingertips had wrinkled, and the skin around the wound had gone a deathly white. There was the odd smear of blood on the hotel dressing gown, but for the most part the bleeding had stopped. My face was pink and childlike. The edges of my skin looked ragged. Jessica had my arm pinned to the bedside table, my damaged hand underneath a small green lamp. She wore her glasses, which was a rarity, and was using tiny tweezers to remove the splinters of wood she had missed the first time, so small that I could barely see. I felt so light that if her hand were not there I would float away and bounce gently off the panelled ceiling.

Does it hurt?

Not even slightly.

Stupid question. I saw you take those tramadol. I'm not an idiot.

Of course you're not an idiot. Would you like some?

Jessica stopped and thought for a moment. After I've done this.

I watched her with heavy-lidded eyes as she removed the pieces of wood, and cleaned the wound with an antiseptic wipe. I did not feel the sting – she may have seen the tramadol, but she did not see me take the hydrocodone (a gift from clearing out Hetty's bathroom). Oh, the poetry of taking my mother's painkillers. I drifted in and out as she applied numbing cream, a dressing pad, and then carefully wound gauze around my hand. She wove in and out of my vision, some kind of dream-dance for my eyes.

My mind dipped in and out of the present and the past, flickering toward my towelled reflection in the mirror and then back inward to making tea for Hetty with two teabags and taking it to her across that thick carpet, a carpet I now had to wade through up to my thighs. I could see Michael drinking tea at the table and Hetty trying to be nice to him and I wondered whether she was really trying, whether those were actually her very best days. I could see myself getting up from the bedside table and pouring whiskey into those little glasses you get in the bathrooms of hotels and handing one to Jess and cheersing her. I could see Hetty pat my wrist across the pitch pine table, and I could see myself weaving around the hotel room, dropping the robe and standing there in my underwear, pulling my boxers down at the back and examining the black bruise forming the shape of Africa across my coccyx.

I did not see the mess I made when I began to knock things off the tables in the hotel room, nor did I see the shards of glass I left when I threw my whiskey at the toilet. I did not see Jessica clean it all up after I had finally fallen unconscious. I did not see her roll the slack weight of me into the recovery position in the bed nor did I see her eyes fill with tears as she placed the wastepaper bin next to me in case I vomited in the night.

I thought about my father. The more I tried to think of Hetty the more I saw my father. Dreaming or awake, he was always running and he would never be fast enough. *We are walking through the market and we break out into the sunshine. There is sand underneath my feet and I hold my father's hand in mine. I can feel his heavy wristwatch against my fingers as we walk. We are next to the sea and my eyes squint to take in the light and I can see my father's brown eyes. I can hear wings beating.*

We didn't talk on the drive back. It was long enough that the silence began to grow the tension between us, like an elastic band pulled nearly to breaking point, something that was once pliable reduced to brittleness and vulnerability. I knew I'd been a cunt, obviously, that much was a given, especially with a belly full of Jamesons and a handful of prescription meds. Not my prescription. Not Hetty's prescription either. I was more like my mother than I cared to admit.

For the week after we returned from Norfolk, I drove myself to and from the hospice without hearing anything from Jessica. The poet was mostly silent – they'd upped her pain medication again, which often left her slack-jawed and unconscious. There was a lull in the day when they eased off the morphine to try and encourage her to eat, but I could hardly bear to be in the room as her body began to move listlessly in pain. She could speak, when she was like that, although she had begun to refuse food. I brought her a strawberry Calipo each day, like I had when she'd been having chemotherapy. She managed to suck some of the slush down, a bit at a time, if I melted the tube in my hands first. That week I even took my laptop in and worked on the book at her bedside. Rebecca sent me draft contracts. I looked at them but couldn't take anything in. It is a strange feeling, to need to be somewhere, and yet when you're there be rendered totally useless. But I was on standby, awaiting her command. I knew it would not be long now. I booked the next week off work, telling Saoirse why, honestly for once, as I apologised for the short notice. She was gentle and understanding and her lilting accent sounded just a touch like the poet, although I knew they were from different parts of Ireland.

Jessica appeared at the end of that week, slipping silently into the poet's room, and pulling up a chair next to me. She'd brought seedless grapes and a smoothie for me and flapped her hands and shushed me when I tried to apologise.

When I wasn't writing I spent hours scrolling through Google, ceaselessly reading end-of-life blogs and forum pages of women with cancer. I began with just breast cancer, before branching out into ovarian, and then other types. I did not belong there. I was struck by how poisonous these spaces seemed to be. Lots of greetings card style slogans, Live, Laugh, Love type stuff except edited to absorb an existence that involved losing control of one's bowels, losing one's hair. They weren't talking a language I understood, which was all to the good, I suppose, as it wasn't a space I belonged in, but also, they weren't narrating an experience I recognised in the poet. She's such a solitary creature, she would not don a pink t-shirt for anyone, nor would she join groups like this, I was sure. The comfort she sought she found internally, some kind of well within her from which she drew the material for her books, the sharpness of her language was the knife she used to cut herself free from the ties of the world, the warmth of her poetry and prose the only bedding she needed at night. I was projecting all this onto her, of course, as I have so many things since I met her. That night Jessica took me home and offered to stay. I accepted. We didn't talk much, again, for what is there to say?

48.

I picked up the book the poet had lent me that final night. I curled up with it on her old bed in the living room, that I still had not taken back upstairs. It was a slender volume, with those deliciously thin pages you only get in Penguin Modern Classics, bible-like, the type velvety black, the cover paperback and flexible in my fingers.

It told the story of a woman who barely existed. A woman who slipped into my mind through the narrator's deft fingertips, but whom I could not grasp. The woman was eclipsed by the narrator, by the author's deliberate touch. Every time I turned my head to look at her, she disappeared. She was a canvas, a window, a trick of the light. It unsettled me. I finished the book in one sitting, alone next to the fire, uneasy in my skin, wondering how I'd ever found it so impenetrable.

'JOY', the author had written in the front cover, in wild, bold handwriting, next to the poet's first name. I took out my laptop, and began to write.

Chapter 49.

Time.

I received the call just after five in the morning. A similar time to all my previous calls from the poet, calls which had once ignited such excitement in my chest. The moon was out again, mocking. The living room was flooded with its light: I'd not shut the curtains before falling into an erratic sleep. I couldn't hear anything at the other end at first, but I stayed on the line. I awaited my instructions.

Time, she said, softly, her voice broken, barely a chirrup.

I waited.

It's time, she said, more deliberate. Take me to the woods. To the water.

I'm coming.

The moon was full on the night the poet died. I should not say night, really, for it was morning, the break of a new day. But it was an ending, not a beginning, and so I cannot call it morning. I left the house in silence, stopping only to pull on shoes and a coat over the tracksuit bottoms and t-shirt I'd been sleeping in. I drove to the hospice, breaking all the speed limits on the silent, milky roads. When I arrived, I ran inside, the soft leather of my trainers making barely a noise on the laminate floors. I ran past the desk, again empty as it had been on my previous moonlit visit. In the elevator I stared at my own face, certain I could see the lunar glow painted onto my pupils, a ghost tattooed onto my eyes. She knew why I was here. She was watching.

When I reached the poet's room, it was clear she had not had any morphine for some time. Her body curved and twisted in the bed. There was sweat on her forehead, and she looked at me with a clarity I had not seen in weeks.

I wrapped her in a blanket and put her in the wheelchair. She relaxed a little as I did so, but kept trying to talk, whispering what sounded like 'time' and 'enough' over and over. I pushed the chair into the lift and as we descended, I brushed the sweaty strands of hair from the poet's face, kissed her gently. She seemed to calm down a little, she gripped my hand hard. She did not speak again.

The ground was hard with frost on the night that the poet died. The wheels of her chair made tracks in the white grass. I pushed her right to the end, to the trees, to the tiny patch of woodland. It was so bright, achingly so. She kept taking my hand and I kept having to pull it away from her sinewy fingers so that I could push the chair properly. She needed to be by water. I couldn't stop yet.

The hospice garden had a sprawling pond. It separated out into three pools, connected by muddy marshland and reeds. This was where I took Kingfisher. There was a large willow tree next to the water. I lifted her from the chair and laid her on the frozen ground, on top of the white cotton hospice blanket. Her breathing eased. She took my hand again. Her face was turned up to the sky. Some of the strain was gone from it. Her body still moved fitfully, but less so. My breath looked like thick fog next to the soft mist emanating from her. I gripped her fingers in mine, running my other hand down her thin spine, feeling the feathers that sprouted there. The skin of her palm was leathery and thick, the flesh seemed to have disappeared. Her breathing changed: she no longer took in air through her nose, instead her chest threw itself up and down, forcing air into her lungs through her open mouth. I was shivering, but she was hot to the touch. Her chest jumped up and down in rhythm, but soon that became erratic.

I stroked her soft blue feathers. Although they're not really blue, are they? It's all about the angle from which you look at her. It's a phenomenon called structural colouration. She is iridescent. She is not what she seems. We lay trembling in the hoarfrost for maybe an hour, until she finally stopped breathing.

50.

The world folded in on itself. I do not know now whether what I remember is the truth or my imaginings. All I have is the pages of the book. There was a funeral, which I did not attend. Pieces on the news, clips from old interviews where her face was framed with curls. A reading of the will – the flat was mine. Jessica moved in with me and decorated, the white walls gained colour, the cold counters gained objects. *Kingfisher* was published the following year, and I won two rather prestigious awards, one which came with a large sum of money. The book sold well, far better than even Rebecca had been expecting. I was *the authority* on the poet. I was often asked to talk about her but rarely accepted. Rebecca invited me to parties and events and I attended some of them. I went on holiday to Mexico with Jessica. I took a permanent position at a university, a different one. The big-name writers were all men. I did not try to fuck any of them.

We kept the painting of the swallow; I do not know what happened to the arctic tern. I do not know what happened to so many things. I was endlessly sweeping blue feathers from the floor. The more I swept them away, the more they appeared.